大学英语选修教材

The Software of the European Mind

西方文化

张纹祯　李景琦　孙　晓　主编

图书在版编目(CIP)数据

西方文化:汉英对照/张纹祯,李景琦,孙晓主编.—天津:天津大学出版社,2010.8
大学英语选修教材
ISBN 978-7-5618-3619-4

Ⅰ.①西…　Ⅱ.①张…②李…③孙…　Ⅲ.①英语-高等学校-教材②西方文化-高等学校-教材　Ⅳ.①H31

中国版本图书馆CIP数据核字(2010)第143239号

出版发行　天津大学出版社
出 版 人　杨欢
地　　址　天津市卫津路92号天津大学内(邮编:300072)
电　　话　发行部:022-27403647　邮购部:022-27402742
网　　址　www.tjup.com
印　　刷　河北省昌黎县第一印刷厂
经　　销　全国各地新华书店
开　　本　148mm×210mm
印　　张　4.25
字　　数　178千
版　　次　2010年8月第1版
印　　次　2010年8月第1次
印　　数　1-5 000
定　　价　15.00元

前　言

为了适应我国高等教育发展的新形势，深化大学公共英语课程的教学改革，提高教学质量，满足新时期国家和社会对人才培养的需要及国际交流的需要，提高大学生英语语言综合应用能力，特别是提高文化素养，天津大学文法学院大学英语教学二部增加了特色精品课程的比重，面向全校各非英语专业本科二年级学生，于第三学期开设这门公共英语选修课。

本书主要介绍两希文化（Greek & Hebrew），帮助学生了解西方文化起源、人文主义思想等，分10单元学习，每单元安排有常识预习、专题讲座、复习反馈和自主拓展四个项目，使学生通过一个学期的学习对西方文化是在希腊文化基础上吸收希伯来文化形成、发展起来的文化背景有一定的了解，增加学生相关的信息量和词汇量，提高英语水平，激发学生的文化学习热情，增长知识、开阔眼界；同时，大家通过学习培养宽容地对待异国文化的态度。

大英二部选修教材建设项目组

目　录

Unit One

warming-up 常识预习

1. What countries are included in "the West"?

2. What are the two major cultural influences over the European mind?

3. What civilization have the Crusades brought into Western culture?

4. Talk about something you know of the West-East contrast during the Cold War.

5. What can be represented by a Celtic knot symbol?

6. Can you give some examples of English terms with Greek or Latin roots?

lecturette 专题讲座

West Is West

It is impossible to embrace the cultures of the entire Western civilization between the covers of one book, we have endeavored to make a reasonably balanced selection.

By *The Software of the European Mind* we refer to cultures of European origin, or simply Western Culture, which implies a Greco-Roman and Judeo-Christian cultural influence, concerning literary, philosophic, artistic and scientific themes and traditions, as well as the cultural social effects of Germanic migration. A Biblical cultural influence in spiritual thinking, customs and either ethic or moral traditions has been further developed during the Middle Ages, so has an ancient Greek civilization during the Renaissance.

Our stereotyped view of "the West" has not been labeled geographically. "The West" today would normally be said to include Europe as well as Japan, the developed countries.

The Classical West

The Greeks felt they were civilized and saw themselves as something between the wild barbarians of most of Europe and the slavish Easterners. Ancient Greek science, philosophy, democracy, architecture, literature, and art provided a foundation embraced and built upon by the Roman Empire as it swept up Europe, including the Hellenic World in its conquests in the 1st century BC. In the meantime, however, Greece, under Alexander, had become a capital of the East, and part of an empire. The idea that the later Orthodox or Eastern Christian cultural descendants of the Greek-speaking Eastern Roman empire are a happy mean between Eastern slavishness and Western barbarism is promoted to this day, creating a zone which is both Eastern and Western depending upon the context of discussion.

For about five hundred years, the Roman Empire maintained the Greek East and consolidated a Latin West, but an East-West division remained, reflected in many cultural norms of the two areas, including language. Eventually the empire came to be increasingly officially split into a Western and Eastern part, reviving old ideas of a contrast between an advanced East, and a rugged West.

With the rise of Christianity in the midst of the Roman world, much of

Rome's tradition and culture were absorbed by the new religion, and transformed into something new, which would serve as the basis for the development of Western civilization after the fall of Rome. Also, Roman culture mixed with the pre-existing Celtic, Germanic and Slavic cultures, which slowly became integrated into Western culture starting, mainly, with their acceptance of Christianity.

The Medieval West

The Medieval West included at its broadest both the "Latin" or "Frankish" West, and the Orthodox Eastern part, where Greek remained the language of empire. More narrowly, it was Catholic (Latin) Europe. After the crowning of Charlemagne, this part of Europe was referred to by its neighbors in Byzantium and the Moslem world as "Frankish".

After the fall of Rome much of Greco-Roman art, literature, science and even technology were all but lost in the western part of the old empire, centered around Italy, and Gaul (France). However, this would become the center of a new West. Europe fell into political anarchy, with many warring kingdoms and principalities. Under the Frankish kings, it eventually reunified and evolved into feudalism.

Much of the basis of the post-Roman cultural world had been set before the fall of the Empire, mainly through the integrating and reshaping of Roman ideas through Christian thought. The Greek and Roman gods had been completely replaced by Christianity around the 4th and 5th centuries, since it became the official State religion as a unifying force in Western Europe. Art and literature, law, education, and politics were preserved in the teachings of the Church. The Church founded many cathedrals, universities, monasteries and seminaries, some of which continue to exist today. In the Medieval period, the route to power for many men was in the Church.

In a broader sense, the Middle Ages, monotheism was not confined to the West but also stretched into the old East, in what was to become the Islamic world, which made its way back to Western Europe via Spain and Italy.

In the Catholic or Frankish west, the Roman law became the foundation on which all legal concepts and systems were based. Its influence can be traced to this day in all Western legal systems (although in different manners and to different extents in the common (Anglo-American) and the civil (continental European) legal traditions). The ideas of civil rights, equality before the law, equality of women, procedural justice, and democracy as the ideal form of society, were principles which formed the basis of modern Western culture.

The West actively encouraged the spreading of Christianity, which was inexorably linked to the spread of Western culture. Owing to the influence of Islamic culture, Western Europeans translated many Arabic texts into Latin during the Middle Ages. Later, with the fall of Constantinople and the Ottoman conquest of the Byzantine Empire, followed by a massive exodus of Greek Christian priests and scholars to Italian towns like Venice, bringing with them as many scripts from the Byzantine archives as they could, scholars' interest in the Greek language and classic works, topics and lost files was revived. Both the Greek and Arabic influences eventually led to the beginnings of the Renaissance. From the late 15th century to the 17th century, Western culture began to spread to other parts of the world by intrepid explorers and missionaries during the Age of Discovery, followed by imperialists from the 17th century to the early 20th century.

The Modern West

As religion became less important, and Europeans came into increasing contact with faraway peoples, the old concept of Western Culture began a slow evolution towards what it is today. The Early Modern "Age of Discovery" in the 15th, 16th and 17th centuries faded into the "Age of Enlightenment" continuing into the 18th, both characterized by the military advantages coming to Europeans from their development of firearms and other military technologies. The "Great Divergence" became more pronounced, making the West the bearer of science and the accompanying revolutions of technology and industrialization. Western political thinking also eventually spread in many forms around the world. With the early 19th century "Age of Revolution" the West entered a period of World empires, massive economic and technological advance, and bloody international conflicts continuing into the 20th century.

Religion in the meantime has waned considerably in Western Europe, where many are agnostic or atheist. Nearly half of the populations of the United Kingdom (44%—54%), Germany (41%—49%), France (43%—54%) and the Netherlands (39%—44%) are non-theist. However, religious belief in the United States is very strong, about 75%—85% of the population, as also happens in most of Latin America.

As Europe discovered the wider world, old concepts adapted. The Islamic world which had formerly been considered "the Orient" ("the East") more specifically became the "Near East" as the interests of the European powers for the first time interfered with Qing China and Meiji Japan in the 19th century.

During the Cold War, the West-East contrast became synonymous with the competing governments of the United States and the Soviet Union and their allies.

Despite the Western empires in the past, concepts of democracy and an emphasis on freedom have been seen as distinguishing Western peoples from non-western neighbors.

In the Middle Ages and early modern times, the concept of a separation of Church and state developed, allowing for the development of more distinctive political norms, such as the doctrine of the separation of powers, which make modern Western democracy distinct from democracy in general.

Cultural Cases

Dance, music, story-telling, and architecture are human universals, and they are expressed in the West in certain characteristic ways.

The symphony has its origins in Italy. Many important musical instruments used by cultures all over the world were also developed in the West; among them are the violin, piano, pipe organ, saxophone, trombone, and clarinet. The solo piano, symphony orchestra and the string quartet are also important performing musical forms.

The ballet is a distinctively Western form of performance dance. The ballroom dance is an important Western variety of dance for the elite. The polska, the square dance, and the Irish step dance are very well-known Western forms of folk dance.

Historically, the main forms of western music are European folk, choral, classical, Country, rock and roll, and hip-hop.

The arch, the dome, and the flying buttress as architectural motifs were first used by the Romans. Important western architectural motifs include the Doric, Corinthian, and Ionic columns, and the Romanesque, Gothic, Baroque, and Victorian styles are still widely recognized, and used even today, in the West. Much of Western architecture emphasizes repetition of simple motifs, straight lines and expansive, undecorated planes. A modern ubiquitous architectural form that emphasizes this characteristic is the skyscraper, first developed in New York and Chicago.

In art, the Celtic knot is a very distinctive Western repeated motif.

Depictions of the nude human male and female in photography, painting and sculpture are frequently considered to have special artistic merit. Realistic portraiture is especially valued. In Western dance, music, plays and other arts, the performers are only very infrequently masked. There are essentially no taboos against depicting God, or other religious figures, in a representational fashion.

Widespread usage of terms and specific vocabulary borrowed or derived from or based on Greek and Latin roots or etymologies for almost any field of arts, science and human knowledge, becoming easily understandable and common to almost any European language, and being a source for inventing internationalized neologisms for nearly any purpose.

Graeco-Roman and Judeo-Christian：两希文化（Greek & Hebrew）

Renaissance：文艺复兴

barbarians：蛮族（未开化的 violent and not educated）

Charlemagne：查理大帝（742—814），神圣罗马帝国的开国皇帝（公元800加冕）

all but：almost

anarchy：no government

inexorable：impossible to stop

Meiji Japan：明治时代的日本

motif：theme, pattern

ubiquitous：present everywhere

polska：a folk dance, common in Nordic countries

going-over 复习反馈

multiple-choice Q's

1. What integrated the Celtic, Germanic and Slavic cultures with the Roman culture into Western culture?

A. The acceptance of Christianity. B. Greece under Alexander.

C. Latin language.

2. Who reunified many warring kingdoms after the fall of Rome?

A. Gaul. B. Charlemagne. C. King Byzas.

3. The ______ influence(s) led to the beginnings of the Renaissance.

A. Greek B. Arabic C. Both A and B

4. Age of Discovery refers to an early modern evolution of the Europe in ______.

A. the 15th century B. the 17th century

C. the 15th, 16th and 17th centuries

5. Religious belief in ______ is very strong.

A. the United Kingdom B. the United States

C. France

6. Which of the following classical style is built with a spiral scroll-like capital?

A. The Doric column. B. The Ionic column.

C. The Corinthian column.

7. ______ is one of the very well-known Western forms of folk dance.

A. Hula B. Polska C. Samba

8. ______ is NOT an example of the modern West skyscrapers.

A. Taipei 101 B. 30 St. Mary Axe

C. The Willis Tower

9. What country looks like a boot at the map?

A. Britain. B. Italy. C. Norway.

essay Q's

10. What are the distinguishing characteristics of the classical West?

11. What role did the Church play in the Middle Ages?

12. What ideas were principles which formed the basis of modern Western culture?

assignments 课题作业

Prepare a brief summary on the cultures of European origin.

This assignment may be presented either as a written text or orally in class next time.

extensions 自主拓展

Learn after-class the European werewolf legends.

This text is included mainly as entertainment. Can you find similar legends in Chinese?

Werewolf legends are widespread in the West. According to them, many people possessed this kind of magical power to transform themselves into wolves by putting on a wolf belt.

Once the huntsmen organized a fox hunt and had placed a dead horse in the woods as bait for the foxes. The werewolf went there and was eating from the horse. The huntsmen surprised him and shot at him. He fled, and when they went to the house of the man they suspected of being a werewolf, they found him in bed with a bullet wound.

Another story goes like this. A young woman whose husband was often unexplainably absent came to the suspicion that he was a werewolf. One day both were working in the field. The man again left his wife. Suddenly a wolf came forth from the bushes, ran toward her, grabbed her red woolen skirt with its teeth and shook her back and forth. With screams and blows from her hay fork she drove him away. Soon afterward her husband emerged from the same bushes into which the wolf had disappeared. She told him of her frightening experience. He laughed, thereby revealing the red woolen threads from her skirt that were stuck between his teeth. She reported him to the judge, and he was burned to death.

Also a woodcutter was working in the forest with his brother. The latter went away, and soon thereafter a wolf came out of the nearby bushes. The woodcutter wounded him on his right front leg with his ax, and the wolf retreated howling. That evening when the woodcutter returned home he found his brother in bed with his right arm hidden beneath the covers. Only after repeated threats would he reveal his arm, and on it was the same wound that the woodcutter had given to the wolf. He reported his brother, who was burned to death, too.

By using a so-called wolf strap, any person could transform himself into a werewolf. Whoever fastened such a strap around himself would turn into a wolf. If someone called out the name of a person who had turned himself into a wolf, that person would regain his human form. In earlier times there were a great many such straps, but today, along with the wolves, they seem to have been banned to Russia.

A wolf strap was a gift from the devil. A person who possessed such a strap could not get rid of it, however much he wanted to. Anyone who accepted a wolf strap also had entered into brotherhood with the devil, surrendering body and soul to him.

If real wolves were feared in earlier times, werewolves were feared all the more. A real wolf could be shot dead or lured into a so-called wolf pit, where it would perish from hunger. However, a werewolf could not be brought down with a rifle bullet, nor would it ever fall into a wolf pit.

What is the use of running around as a werewolf?

This was not done for no good reason. When the pantries and meat containers were empty, one would only have to fasten on the wolf strap, run off as a wolf, seek out a fat sheep that was wandering off toward the edge of the woods, creep towards it, seize it, and drag it into the woods. In the evening one could bring it home without anyone noticing. Or the werewolf would know when a peasant was going through the woods with a lot of money. He would ambush him, rob him, then run off across the field with the booty.

In earlier times, after the horses had been unhitched from a wagon or a plow, they would be driven out to a community pasture where they would be watched until morning by two herdsmen. Even colts were put out for the night. People took turns watching after them.

Now once it happened that one of the two herdsmen had a wolf strap. After both herdsmen had kept watch for several hours they got sleepy and laid their heads down. The first one, however, who had heard that his companion possessed a wolf strap, only pretended to be asleep, and the other one thought that he was indeed sleeping. He quickly fastened the strap around himself and ran off as a wolf. The other one got up and saw how his companion ran up to a colt, attacked it, and devoured it.

After this had happened, the wolf man came back and lay down to sleep. Toward morning they both awoke. The werewolf man was rolling around on the ground and groaning loudly. The other one asked him what was wrong.

He said that he had a horrible stomach ache.

To this the first one said, "The devil himself would have a stomach ache if he had eaten an entire colt at one time."

A woman can transform herself into a werewolf as well.

In a village there lived a woman. Her husband had been dead for a long time. The woman lived in impoverished circumstances, but nonetheless, she was always able to offer fresh meat to those who visited her.

One time a male relative came to visit her, and she offered him good fresh meat.

The man said to her, "Tell me, where did you get this nice mutton?"

The woman answered, "I'll show you. Just climb up onto the roof with the ladder that is leaning against the back of the house."

The man did what the woman asked him to do. In the distance he saw a herd of sheep. Suddenly a wolf came out of the brush, ran into the midst of the sheep, and was about to run away with one of them. The shepherd saw this in time, and with his dog took off after the wolf in order to rescue the sheep. The wolf defended itself.

The man on the roof, knowing what kind of wolf it was, called out "watch out".

Suddenly the woman was standing there in her true form. Then the shepherd began striking out at her with renewed vigor, and the woman was scarcely able to drag herself back home.

People still believe in werewolves even today in some villages of Europe. Whenever he ties around his body a strip of leather made from wolf skin which still has its hair, such a person could turn himself into a wolf. When the leather strip would be taken off, or his name would be shouted out on the spot, he would become a reasonable human once again.

---

werewolf：狼人

Unit Two

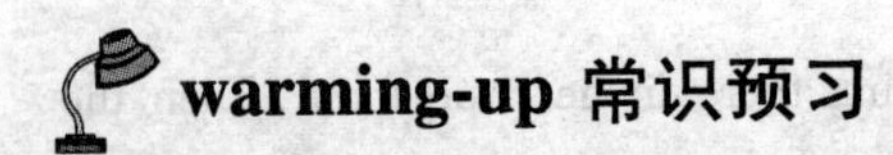

warming-up 常识预习

1. Do you know the story of Persephone (Proserpine) and pomegranate?

2. *Prometheus Bound*, *Oedipus the king*, *Medea and Andromache*, are well known Greek plays. Who wrote them?

3. Did Greek women do housework themselves?

4. Is Pythagoras the founder of scientific mathematics?

5. As for Greek Orders (or types of column), which one is sturdy and shaped like a man? Which is topped with scrolls like curls of hair of a woman?

6. What landmark of Greece was dedicated to the Goddess Athena (built on the Acropolis of Athens)?

lecturette 专题讲座

The Greek Culture

The ancient Greeks loved stories. They created many marvelous stories, myths, and fables that we enjoy today, like *Odysseus* and *The Terrible Sea and Circe*, a beautiful but evil enchantress. *Aesop's Fables* are still read and enjoyed all over the world, as well as plays written by the greatest tragic dramatists of ancient Greece: Aeschylus, Sophocles, and Euripides. The Greeks worshipped many gods who they believed appeared in human form and yet were endowed with superhuman strength and ageless beauty. *The Iliad* (describing the war led by Agamemnon against the city of Troy) and *The Odyssey*, their earliest surviving examples of Greek literature, record men's interactions with various gods and goddesses whose characters and appearances underwent little change in the centuries that followed. Various painted scenes on vases, and stone, terracotta and bronze sculptures portray the major gods and goddesses. The deities were depicted either by themselves or in traditional mythological situations in which they interact with humans and a broad range of minor deities, demi-gods and legendary characters. Aphrodite was the only Goddess to ever be portrayed in the nude. In 530 BC naked women were a hot topic for vases. These women were portrayed in very suggestive and lewd positions.

Early Greek burials were frequently marked above ground by a large piece of pottery, and remains were also buried in urns. Pottery continued to be used extensively inside tombs and graves throughout the classical period. The two-handled loutrophoros was primarily associated with weddings, as it was used to carry water for the nuptial bath. However, it was also placed in the tombs of the unmarried, "presumably to make up in some way for what they had missed in life". The one-handled lekythos had many household uses, but outside the household its principal use was for decoration of tombs. Scenes of a descent to the underworld of Hades were often painted on these. Small pottery figurines are often found, though it is hard to decide if these were made especially for placing in tombs.

Men ran the government, and spent a great deal of their time away from home. When not involved in politics, the men spent time in the fields, overseeing or working the crops, sailing, hunting, in manufacturing or in trade. For fun, in addition to drinking parties, the men enjoyed wrestling, horseback riding, and the famous Olympic Games. The Olympic Games were first held in Olympia in 776 BC when athletes competed naked. The Games were to honor the gods, Zeus and Hera. (The Olympics were revived in 1896 in Athens and held there again in 2004. The Olympics take place every four years.) When the men entertained their male friends, at the popular drinking parties, their wives and daughters were not allowed to attend. With the exception of ancient Sparta, Greek women had very limited freedom outside the home. They could attend weddings, funerals, some religious festivals, and could visit female neighbors for brief periods of time. In their home, Greek women were in charge. Their job was to run the house and to bear children. Most Greek women did not do housework themselves. Most Greek households had slaves. Female slaves cooked, cleaned, and worked in the fields. Male slaves watched the door, to make sure no one came in when the man of the house was away, except for female neighbors, and acted as tutors to the young male children. Wives and daughters were not allowed to watch the Olympic Games as the participants in the games did not wear clothes. Chariot racing was the only game women could win, and only then if they owned the horse. If that horse won, they received the prize.

The ancient Greeks considered their children to be "youths" until they reached the age of 30! When a child was born to ancient Greek family, a naked father carried his child, in a ritual dance, around the household. Friends and relatives sent gifts. The family decorated the doorway of their home with a wreath of olives (for a boy) or a wreath of wool (for a girl). In Athens, as in most Greek city-states, with the exception of Sparta, girls stayed at home until they were married. Like their mother, they could attend certain festivals, funerals, and visit neighbors for brief periods of time. Their job was to help their mother, and to help in the fields, if necessary. Ancient Greek children played with many toys, including rattles, little clay animals, horses on 4 wheels that could be pulled on a string, yo-yo's, and terracotta dolls.

Education in the Greek city-states was to prepare the child for adult activities as a citizen. The nature of the city-states varied greatly, and this was also true of the education they considered appropriate. In most Greek city-states, when young, the boys stayed at home, helping in the fields, sailing, and fishing. At age 6 or 7, they went to school. Both daily life and education were very different as in Sparta—militant, than in Athens—arts and culture.

The goal of education in Sparta, was to produce soldier-citizens who were well-drilled, well-disciplined marching army. Spartans believed in a life of discipline, self-denial, and simplicity. Spartan boys were sent to military school at age 7. At school, they were taught survival skills and only warfare mattered. The boys were not fed well, and were told that it was fine to steal food as long as they did not get caught stealing. If they were caught, they were beaten. They walked barefoot, slept on hard beds, and worked at gymnastics and other physical activities such as running, jumping, javelin and discus throwing, swimming, and hunting. But the typical Spartan may not have been able to read. Somewhere between the ages of 18 – 20, Spartan males had to pass a difficult test of fitness, military ability, and leadership skills. Any Spartan male who did not pass these examinations became a perioikos. If they passed, they became a full citizen and a Spartan soldier. Spartan citizens were not allowed to touch money. That was the job of the middle class. They ate, slept, and continued to train in their brotherhood barracks. Even if they were married, they did not live with their wives and families. They lived in the barracks. Military service did not end until a Spartan male reached the age of 60. Then a Spartan soldier could retire and live in their home with their family. Unlike the other Greek city-states, Sparta provided training for girls that went beyond the domestic arts. The girls were not forced to leave home, but otherwise their training was similar to that of the boys. They too learned to run, jump, throw the javelin and discus, and wrestle mightiest strangle a bull. Girls also went to school at age 7. They lived, slept and trained in their sisterhood's barracks where the girls were taught wrestling, gymnastics and combat skills. The Spartans believed that strong young women would produce strong babies. At age 18, if a Sparta girl passed her skills and fitness test, she would be assigned a husband and allowed to return home. If she failed, she would lose her rights as a citizen, and became a perioikos. In Sparta, citizen women were free to move around, and enjoyed a great deal of freedom, as their husbands did not live at home.

The goal of education in Athens, a democratic city-state, was to produce citizens trained in the arts of both peace and war. The word "democracy" comes from the Greek "demos", which means people and "krakos", which means power. In the 5th century, Athens was a democracy. Athens' leaders, rather than inheriting power or even seizing it, were elected by its' people or citizens. The schools were private, but the tuition was low enough so that even the poorest citizens could afford to send their children for at least a few years. Until age 6 or 7, boys were generally taught at home by their mothers. Most Athenian girls had a primarily domestic education. The most highly educated women were the hetaerae, or courtesans, who attended special schools where they learned to be interesting companions for the men who could afford to maintain them. Boys attended elementary schools from the time they were about age 7 until they were 14. Part of their training was gymnastics. Younger boys learned to move gracefully, do calisthenics, and play ball and other games. The older boys learned running, jumping, boxing, wrestling, and discus and javelin throwing. The boys also learned to play the lyre and sing, to count, and to read and write. As soon as their pupils could write, the teachers dictated passages from Homer for them to take down, memorize, and later act out. The wealthier boys continued their education under the tutelage of philosopher-teachers. Until about 390 BC there were no permanent schools and no formal courses for such higher education. Gradually, as groups of students attached themselves to one teacher or another, permanent schools were established. It was in such schools that Plato, Socrates, and Aristotle taught. The boys who attended these schools fell into more or less two groups. Those who wanted learning for its own sake studied with philosophers like Plato who taught such subjects as geometry, astronomy, harmonics, and arithmetic. Those who wanted training for public life studied with philosophers like Socrates who taught primarily oratory and rhetoric. In democratic Athens such training was appropriate and necessary because power rested with the men who had the ability to persuade their fellow senators to act.

Greek Culture reached a high point of development in the 5th century B. C., and in 146 B. C., the Romans conquered Greece. However, the "captive Greece took her rude conqueror captive". Greek culture exercised the heavy influence over English literature.

Byron dreamt

"The isles of Greece! the isles of Greece!

Where burning Sappho loved and sung,

Where grew the arts of war and peace,... "

Shelley saw hope in *Prometheus Unbound* where the old views of good and evil needed a change.

Keats sang for a Grecian Urn,

"Beauty is truth, truth beauty."

The sun is new everyday, so we can not step twice into the same river.

That's why D. H. Lawrence said we are liars about love, "the truth of yesterday becomes a lie tomorrow".

And Freud even found the Oedipus complex in the child's life.

---

be endowed with: to have a good ability or quality

Hades: 冥王(哈得斯 lord of the underworld),Zeus 的哥哥,罗马名字 Pluto

terracotta: brown-red clay

perioikos: a member of the middle class, allowed to own property, have business dealings, but had no political rights and were not citizens

harmonics: the mathematical theory of music

going-over 复习反馈

multiple-choice Q's

1. Which of the following pieces of pottery would be used to carry bathwater during a wedding?

A. Lekythos B. Urn C. Loutrophoros

2. _______ were among many toys with which the Greek children played.

A. Sparta birds, chariots, and wooden horses

B. Rattles, yo-yo's and little clay animals

C. Barbie girls, slaves and terracotta dolls

3. Democracy began in _______.

A. Athens B. Troy C. Sparta

4. What did boys in Athens learn at school?

A. Running and boxing, reading and writing and so on.

B. Jumping and discus throwing, swimming, and hunting and so on.

C. Gymnastics and combat skills, wrestling and singing and so on.

5. When did a Greek family decorate the doorway of their home with a wreath?

A. When they dreamt scenes of a descent to the underworld.

B. When a family member died.

C. When a child was born to the family.

6. The Spartans believed that ______.

A. power rested with the men who had the ability to persuade their fellow senators to act

B. strong young women would produce strong babies

C. the truth of yesterday becomes a lie tomorrow

7. Who was the founder of the Academy in Athens, the first school of higher learning in the western world?

A. Socrates. B. Plato. C. Aristotle.

8. ______ is the Greek goddess of fertility.

A. Isis B. Frigga C. Aphrodite

9. ______ described a journey home.

A. *Prometheus Unbound* B. *The Iliad*

C. *The Odyssey*

essay Q's

10. What did Greek men enjoy for fun?

11. Exemplify the influence of Greek culture on English literature.

12. Tell about the Greek hero of the movie *Clash of the Titans*.

assignments 课题作业

Prepare a brief summary on the education in Sparta and in Athens. This assignment may be presented either as a written text or orally in class next time.

extensions 自主拓展

Learn after-class the tales from "Aesop's Fables".

This text is included mainly as entertainment. What are the morals of these tales?

Wolf! Wolf!

There once was a boy who kept sheep not far from the village. He would often become bored and to amuse himself he would call out, "Wolf! Wolf," although there was no wolf about. The villagers would stop what they were doing and run to save the sheep from the wolf's jaw. Once they arrived at the pasture, the boy just laughed. The naughty boy played this joke over and over until the villagers tired of him. One day while the boy was watching the sheep, a wolf did come into the fold. The boy cried and cried, "Wolf! Wolf!" No one came. The wolf had a feast of sheep that day.

The Fox said the Grapes Must Be Sour

A very hungry fox walked into a vineyard where there was an ample supply of luscious looking grapes. Grapes had never looked so good, and the fox was famished. However, the grapes hung higher than the fox could reach. He jumped and stretched and hopped and reached and jumped some more trying to get those yummy grapes, but to no avail. No matter what he tried, he could not reach the grapes. He wore himself out jumping and jumping to get the grapes. "Those grapes surely must be sour," he said as he walked away, "I wouldn't eat them if they were served to me on a silver platter."

The Tortoise Challenged the Hare to a Race

One day a hare was bragging about how fast he could run. He bragged and bragged and even laughed at the tortoise, who was so slow. The tortoise stretched out his long neck and challenged the hare to a race, which, of course, made the hare laugh. "My, my, what a joke!" thought the hare. "A race, indeed, a race. Oh! what fun! My, my! a race, of course, Mr. Tortoise, we shall race!" said the hare. The forest animals met and mapped out the course. The race begun, and the hare, being such a swift runner, soon left the tortoise far behind. About halfway through the course, it occurred to the hare that he had plenty of time to beat the slow trodden tortoise. "Oh, my!" thought the hare, "I have plenty of time to play in the meadow here." And so he did. After the hare finished playing, he decided that he had time to take a little nap. "I have plenty of time to beat that tortoise," he thought. And he cuddled up against a tree and dozed. The tortoise, in the meantime, continued to plod on, albeit, it ever so slowly. He never stopped, but took one good step after another. The hare finally woke from his nap. "Time to get going," he thought. And off he went faster than he had ever run before! He dashed as quickly as anyone ever could up to the finish line, where he met the tortoise, who was patiently awaiting his arrival.

The Wolf in Sheep's Clothing

Once upon a time a Wolf resolved to disguise his appearance in order to secure food more easily. Encased in the skin of a sheep, he pastured with the flock deceiving the shepherd by his costume. In the evening he was shut up by the shepherd in the fold; the gate was closed, and the entrance made thoroughly secure. But the shepherd, returning to the fold during the night to obtain meat for the next day, mistakenly caught up the Wolf instead of a sheep, and killed him instantly.

The Country Mouse and the City Mouse

A country mouse invited his cousin who lived in the city to come to visit him. The city mouse was so disappointed with the sparse meal which was nothing more than a few kernels of corn and a couple of dried berries. "My poor cousin," said the city mouse, "you hardly have anything to eat! I do believe that an ant could eat better! Please do come to the city and visit me, and I will show you such rich feasts, readily available for the taking." So the country mouse left with his city cousin who brought him to a splendid feast in the city's alley. The country mouse could not believe his eyes. He had never seen so much food in one place. There was bread, cheese, fruit, cereals, and grains of all sorts scattered about in a warm cozy portion of the alley. The two mice settled down to eat their wonderful dinner, but before they barely took their first bites, a cat approached their dining area. The two mice scampered away and hid in a small uncomfortable hole until the cat left. Finally, it was quiet, and the unwelcome visitor went to prowl somewhere else. The two mice ventured out of the hole and resumed their abundant feast. Before they could get a proper taste in their mouth, another visitor intruded on their dinner, and the two little mice had to scuttle away quickly. "Goodbye," said the country mouse, "You do, indeed, live in a plentiful city, but I am going home where I can enjoy my dinner in peace."

The Lion's Share

The lion went hunting one day with three other beasts. Together, they surrounded and caught a deer. With the consent of the other three, the lion divided the prey into four equal shares, but just when each animal was about to take his portion, the lion stopped them. "Wait," said the lion, "Since I am a member of the hunting party, I am to receive one of these portions. Since I am considered to rank so high among the beasts of the forest, I am to receive the second share. Since I am known for my courage and strength, I am to receive the third share. As for the fourth share, if you wish to argue with me about its ownership, let's begin, and we will see who will get it."

The North Wind and the Sun

The North Wind and the Sun were disputing which was the stronger, when a traveler came along wrapped in a warm cloak. They agreed that the one who first succeeded in making the traveler take his cloak off should be considered stronger than the other. Then the North Wind blew as hard as he could, but the more he blew the more closely did the traveler fold his cloak around him; and at last the North Wind gave up the attempt. Then the Sun shined out warmly, and immediately the traveler took off his cloak. And so the North Wind was obliged to confess that the Sun was the stronger of the two.

---

on a silver platter: 轻而易举

Unit Three

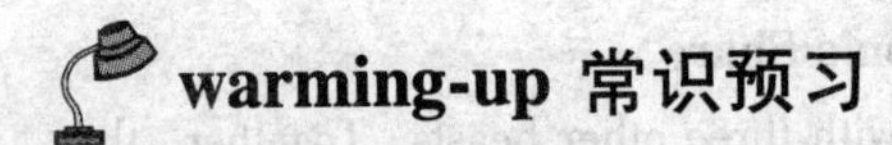

warming-up 常识预习

1. Who wrote “I came, I saw, I conquered”(拉丁原文 veni, vidi, vici,亲临、目睹、全胜)?

2. For what epic is Virgil known?

3. What did the Romans construct throughout the empire for water supply?

4. An elliptical amphitheatre in the center of the city of Rome is the largest ever built in the Roman Empire. What is it called?

5. Peiyang University, now Tianjin University, was founded in 1895, the year in Roman numerals is written as ________________。

6. Know some proverbs about Rome.

lecturette 专题讲座

Pax Romana

Latin, an Indo-European language, was written in an alphabet derived from the Greek alphabet, and Greek from the one made by the Phoenicians, with some letters changed. English-speakers have added the letters J and U and W. The Romans only used what is called capital (upper case) letters in modern usage. And Roman numerals based on letters of the alphabet remained in common use until about the 14th century in Europe. Nearly all of the Latin literature that we still have today survives because it was copied over and over by hand by different people through hundreds of years. Two major language groups were spoken in the Mediterranean in the ancient and medieval periods. These are Indo-European and Semitic. The Indo-European language group seems to have originated between the Black Sea and the Caspian Sea, in modern Georgia. Around 3000 BC some of the people who spoke this language began to travel away from here. Some of them went west toward the Atlantic Ocean and these are now known as the Celts, and they speak the Celtic languages like Gaelic, Breton, and so on. A little later, others traveled over the Black Sea toward the Mediterranean or south to Western Asia. Some of them settled in Italy, where Indo-European became Latin. Some went north, where Indo-European turned into German, Norwegian, English and so on. The people who stayed more or less where they were in Russia began to speak the Slavic and Baltic languages. The Semitic languages include Hebrew, Arabic, etc. They were spoken mainly along the coast of the Mediterranean Sea. Most likely the language group started out somewhere around Lebanon or Syria, and spread from there eastward and southward. Egyptians split off very early, and is very different from the other Semitic languages. Arabic seems to be the closest to what Semitic languages were like a long time ago and didn't change much.

Around 500 BC, just as democracy was getting started in Athens, the Roman rich people decided they didn't want to be ruled by Etruscan kings anymore. (Romulus ruled as the first King of Rome from 753 to 715 BC. Tarquinius I, the first Etruscan monarch, succeeded Marcius as the fifth King ruling from 616 to 579 BC). The kings were doing okay for the poor people, but the rich people wanted more power for themselves. But the rich people couldn't get rid of the kings all by themselves. They needed the poor men to fight for them. So they promised the poor men that they could have a lot of power in the new government, if they would help get rid of the kings. The poor men agreed to help, and together the Romans threw out the Etruscan kings. But once the kings were out, the Roman aristocrats didn't want to give the poor men any power. So the leaders of the poor men moved outside the city and went on strike. They refused to work any more unless they got some power. The Roman aristocrats had to give in, and they let the poor men, but not the women or slaves, vote. Still the poor men of Rome did not get as much power as the poor men of Athens. Instead of voting about what to do themselves, the Romans voted to choose leaders, who decided for them, the way the United States President and Congress do today. But the only people who could be elected to the Roman Senate were the rich people. After another few years, the poor people of Rome still felt they were not being treated right. They made the aristocrats agree that the poor men could also elect tribunes. Tribunes had to be chosen from the poor people, and they went to all the meetings of the Senate. They could veto anything the Senate did which would be bad for the poor people, and it meant that the tribunes could forbid any law that was bad for the poor.

The poor people also made the aristocrats write down the laws and put them in a public square where anyone could read them (though not very many people could read). These were called *The Twelve Tables*, and this stopped the aristocrats from pretending that there was a law about something when really there was not.

Meanwhile, the Roman army had been little by little conquering the cities around them. Now most people at this time, when they conquered a city, just took all the stuff they wanted, wrecked some buildings, and then went home and left the city alone. But the Romans, when they conquered a city, did something new: they made that city part of the Roman Empire. The people who lived in that city got the right to vote in Rome (at least sometimes), and they paid taxes to Rome, and they sent men to be in the Roman army. Because of this new idea, the more the Romans conquered, the richer they got, and the more men they had in their army, so that it became easier for them to conquer the next city. Soon the Romans had taken over most of the middle of Italy. Now the Romans began to conquer southern Italy. They used another good idea to help them. They told everybody that if any city needed help fighting a war, the Romans would be happy to help them. Soon a city did ask for help, when its neighbors were attacking it. The Romans sent troops and fought off the neighbors. But when the war was over, the Romans announced that they were going to leave Roman soldiers in this city to keep the city safe. But when there are Roman soldiers living in the middle of your city, you pretty much have to do whatever the Roman Senate says! In this way the Romans took over all of southern Italy.

The burning of Corinth in 146 BC marked Roman conquest of Greece. As the Roman soldiers marched through Greece, they saw a lot of Greek art in the temples, and in public squares and people's houses. They brought home a lot of the Greek art they saw either by buying it or by stealing it, or maybe sometimes the Greeks gave it to them for presents, and they also brought back Greek sculptors (often as slaves) to make more art for them in Rome. The Roman art of the first and second centuries AD pretty much continued the traditions of portraiture and Greek imitations. Roman artists added more use of art as propaganda to show what the emperors wanted people to know or to think. They also had a lot of fresco painting to decorate the walls of their houses during this time.

The Roman Empire which covered most of Europe and all around the

Mediterranean could hardly have only one art style all over it. Local people found ways to mix their old art styles with new Roman ideas. First, the wars with the Germans in the north were accompanied by a new taste for bloodshed in art, so that monuments produced in the 200 AD often show people having their heads cut off or their guts ripped out, or suffering in some other way. And there was at the same time a new concern for the soul, maybe because there were more and more Christians in the Roman Empire. In art, this shows up as a lot of emphasis on "the windows to the soul", often with the eyes looking upward to heaven, or toward the gods. Then the body is less important, the sculptors take less care to show the body accurately. Sometimes the arms and legs are too short, and the head tends to be too big.

The city of Rome itself has tremendous environmental advantages, which made it easier for Rome to become an important city. Rome is located at the first place that people can easily cross the Tiber River, so it is the natural location of the main north-south road in Italy. The reason you can cross the Tiber at Rome is that there is an island in the river there. There are also important salt flats near the city, and because salt was so valuable in the ancient world, these were also important to the early city of Rome. Also the riverboats going up and down the Tiber, from east to west and back again, could stop at Rome.

As the Romans expanded their empire, they encountered many different environments. There were mountains, deserts, swamps, forests, and everything else. The Roman army had to learn to fight in different ways in order to conquer these different areas. They had to learn to split up their big legions into small guerrilla units that would be able to get around quickly and quietly in the mountains or in the forest. One reason that the Roman army was so successful that it was able to adapt to changing environments.

During the period about 100 BC to 500 AD, the Romans had the great advantage of controlling the whole Mediterranean Sea. This made trade much easier because people could ship things by boat. They also had the advantage of getting food and materials from lots of different environments. They could get tin from England, and wood from Germany, and cotton from Egypt, and silver from Spain.

In some ways Roman religion is a lot like the Greek, but in other ways it is very different. Like the Greeks, the Romans thought that there were many gods, and that these gods each controlled different parts of the world: storms, the ocean, marriage, blacksmithing, and so forth.

The Romans were particularly interested in contracts, and much less interested in balance than the Greeks. One important Roman idea about their gods was "do ut des", which is Latin for "I give so that you will give". People should sacrifice to the gods, so that the gods would help them in return.

The chief of the gods, for the Romans, was Jupiter, similar to the Greek god Zeus in many ways. They are both sky gods who throw lightning bolts when they are angry. The Roman goddesses Juno and Minerva correspond more or less to the Greek goddesses Hera and Athena. The conquered Africans (with the Egyptians), Europeans, and West Asian people like the Jews continued to worship their own gods, as well as adopting Roman gods. The Roman leaders didn't have any problem with people worshiping as many gods as they liked, although they didn't like it when the Jews and Christians refused to worship Roman gods.

The Romans adopted many Greek gods as their own and began to worship them as well. One early example is the twin gods Castor and Pollux. As the Roman Empire expanded, people also began to worship the gods of other conquered areas, like the Egyptian goddess Isis and the Syrian god

Mithra. And a lot of people living in Rome seem to have believed, also, that having a good image of somebody's face was important to keeping their ghost happy after they died so they wouldn't haunt you. So all the way through the Roman Empire we see a lot of portraits.

Pax Romana: Latin for "Roman peace", a long period lasting 200 years

Phoenicians: 古代腓尼基人,他们造的字母一开始也都是象形的,如:希腊人这样写的A,原来腓尼基人的是倒立过来写的,是牛头,念aleph

fresco: 湿壁画(cheaper than marble panels)

salt flats: dry lakes whose surface is primarily salt 盐滩

tribunes: government officials to protect the rights of ordinary people

veto: "I forbid it" in Latin

The Twelve Tables: 古罗马第一部成文法典,对贵族权力作了限制,据说刻在12块铜牌上,后来高卢人入侵罗马被毁

 going-over 复习反馈

multiple-choice Q's

1. What river was believed to be the river into which Romulus and Remus were thrown as infants?

A. Tiber.　B. Danube.　C. Nile.

2. Which of the following is a Roman goddess?

A. Mithra.　B. Minerva.　C. Athena.

3. Most of the English letters in the alphabet came from ______.

A. Germanic　B. Indo-European　C. Latin

4. The Semitic languages do not include ______.

A. Arabic B. Hebrew C. Baltic

5. The ______ painting was popular in ancient Rome to decorate the walls of their houses.

A. canvas B. fresco C. relief

6. Portraits had been favored by the Romans because ______.

A. they were superstitious B. they were narcissistic

C. they were aristocratic

7. The Romans could get tin from ______ as they expanded their empire.

A. Germany B. Egypt C. England

8. Which of the following Latin mottos means the principle of reciprocity?

A. Domine, dirige nos B. Donna nobis pacem

C. Do ut des

9. The Romans admired the ______ art and had a tradition of imitating it.

A. Greek B. Gaul C. Egyptian

essay Q's

10. How did the Romans make it easier to conquer a city one after another?

11. What did the poor men of Rome do for their democracy?

12. Why did the Roman sculptors take less care to show a human body accurately?

assignments 课题作业

Prepare a brief summary on the rise of the Roman Empire. This assignment may be presented either as a written text or orally in class next time.

extensions 自主拓展

Learn after-class the Romulus and Rome legend. This text is included mainly as entertainment. How does the she-wolf become one of the icons of the founding of Rome?

The history of Rome embraces a very interesting set of events that connect the ancient Greek civilization to the Romans. This is the legend of the she-wolf (Lupa Capitolina), which since the origins of Roma has become the symbol of the city. One thousand years before Christ, the first settlers had come from north of the River Tiber. They were mostly shepherds and agricultural people that had settled in Tuscany during 2 000 BC. At that time, the Etruscans had conquered the entire Lazio.

The great Roman poet, Virgil (70—19 BC), in the book *Aeneid*, beautifully describes the seven-year Odyssey of Aeneas, a Trojan hero, a son by the goddess Venus, by land and sea. After he fled with his family from Greece, Aeneas landed in the River Tiber in central Italy (approximately where the region of Lazio is today). A decade before, in Greece, Aeneas had led the Trojans in their struggle against the Greeks who, after a siege of several years, had entered the city of Troy in the belly of a wooden horse. Aeneas had a very difficult journey: during the crossing of the Mediterranean Sea, he lost his wife Lavinia between Thrace and Crete, then in Sicily his father died. Cast up by a storm, his ship, driven by strong winds, ended up on the African coast. Dido, the queen of Carthage (today's Libya), fell in love with him, but when Aeneas refused to marry her, she killed herself. Aeneas sailed from Africa with his son Ascanius and finally reached the coast of Lazio, seven years after leaving Troy burning like a pyre. They settled in this new land, and after Aeneas died, his son Ascanius founded the city of Alba Longa right on the area where 30 years before he had landed with his father.

A few years later, Rhea Silvia, a name connoting the Great Mother and the forest (Latin: silva), a beautiful Vestal, daughter of Numitor, the rightful king of Alba, had a romance with god Mars and gave birth to twin sons Romulus and Remus. The "Vestals" were virgins who dedicated their lives to keep the sacred fire of Vesta burning 24 hours a day. "Vesta" was the Roman virgin goddess of the hearth, home, and family. The shrine of Vesta stood in the Forum, near the Regia, palace of the kings. The Vestal cult continued for centuries until the Christian Emperor Constantine eliminated the worship of all ancient deities.

Amulius, Numitor's brother, deposed their grandfather and became a new king of Alba, ordered that their mother Rhea Silvia be killed for having lost her virginity, and their great-uncle recognized that her twins, Romulus and Remus, were more than human and attempted to have them drowned in the River Tiber. One of the servants eliminated Rhea Silvia, another one put Romulus and Remus in a small trough, but could not bring himself to throw the twins in the river; instead, he left them near the bank. In the morning, the babies were hungry and crying. A she-wolf happened to go by and her maternal instinct induced her to stop and nurse them. They were rescued by a she-wolf who suckled and cared for them, and a woodpecker, who fed them. Days later the shepherd Faustulus and his wife Larentia, found the babies and picked up the twins and raised them as their own children.

Twenty years later, Romulus and Remus grew up into strong young men, born leaders of the shepherds and outlaws in the surrounding countryside. Remus was captured in a brawl with some of his grandfather's shepherds. Romulus attempted to rescue his brother, and the presence of twins round the right age uncovered the secret. With their own followers and their grandfather's men, they deposed their great-uncle and restored their grandfather to his throne. Romulus and Remus did not want to serve anybody else as king, so they left Alba to found their own city.

They chose different sites, and decided to seek omens for which would be better. Remus looked round and saw six vultures, a good omen, whereupon Romulus claimed to have seen twelve, even better. While they were arguing, Remus jumped contemptuously over the walls Romulus had built. Romulus was made even angrier by this, and in a fit of rage, killed his brother. Romulus buried Remus, and carried on with building his city. There was one problem: all the inhabitants, being shepherds, runaway slaves and brigands, were men. Romulus held games in honor of the god Consus, and invited people from the Sabine communities roundabout. While they were watching the games, Romulus gave a signal and the Romans seized the young Sabine women who were attending the games and made off with them. The Sabines later tried to get the women back, but by this time they had married their abductors and some of them had become mothers. The women interposed themselves between the two armies, and pleaded not to be forced to choose between their relatives by blood and their relatives by marriage. Peace was restored and Romulus and Tatius, the king of the Sabines, were made joint monarchs. Tatius was killed after only five years, and Romulus then reigned alone. After having reigned over Rome for 38 years, Romulus disappeared in a violent storm, and it was announced that he had been taken up to heaven, from where he would continue to look after Rome's destiny as the god Quirinus.

The founding of the city was carefully tied into history. The Roman historian Livy (late 1st century B. C.) wrote his history giving dates AUC (ab urbe condita = from the founding of the city). His history starts with the founding of Rome. Plutarch, a Greek biographer of the early 2nd century A. D., wrote a biography of Romulus in which he dates the founding of Rome by referring to eclipses observed in Greece. He also mentions attempts to historicize the information by interpreting the she-wolf as a prostitute and Mars as someone dressed up to fool their mother (Plutarch Romulus). For the Romans, the supernatural details did not detract from the historicity of the events.

Lupa Capitolina: the bronze wolf found on the ancient Capitoline Hill, caring for the twins Romulus and Remus

Toscany: 托斯卡纳(意大利的最美丽的地区,如今已有 6 处被列为世界遗产)

Etruscans: 伊特鲁斯坎人(最早在台伯河流域建立文明,后被罗马同化)

Lazio: 拉齐奥(罗马政府所在地区,意大利语,拉丁语为 Latium)

Sabines: 萨宾人(与拉丁人共同创立古罗马文明的部族)

Unit Four

warming-up 常识预习

1. How many stories did the Tower of Babel have?
2. Who is Moses?
3. Where is Babylon?
4. Of how many books does the *Bible* consist?
5. Is Star of David the same as Solomon's Seal?
6. When was Christianity broken into two big churches?

An Eye for an Eye

By the Hebrew culture we usually refer to the *Bible* and Christianity part of the western civilization. In the 6th century BC in Babylon the Hebrews formed synagogues to practice their religion. A synagogue was a Jewish house of assembly or prayer, a large social hall with smaller rooms or offices for "schul" (a Yiddish term in everyday speech in English-speaking countries, study). The Hebrew word for priest is kohen. And their Menorah is a seven-branched candelabrum; Hanukkah, eight-branched for Festival of Lights. As a matter of history, Babylon is often talked about. The title expression "an eye for an eye" is a saying from the Code of Hammurabi, inscribed on a stone 1760 BC at Old Babylonia, an ancient city-state. This was the Mesopotamia period. And it is said that the Great Flood was there about 2370 BC. While the well-known poem "Waters of Babylon" referred to Neo-Babylonian Empire period of the 6th century BC. "By the rivers of Babylon..." has been set to music on several occasions. It describes the sadness of the Israelites, asked to sing the Lord's song in a foreign land.

"By the rivers of Babylon,
there we sat down, yeah we wept
when we remembered Zion.
For there they carried us away in captivity,
requiring of us a song.
Now how shall we sing the lord's song
in a strange land.
Let the words of our mouths and the meditations of our hearts
be acceptable in the sight here tonight.
..."

However, they built the Hanging Gardens and the 7 storey Tower (91 m high Babel, Hebrew name for Babylon). The Genesis has a different story of the Tower. A mighty hunter called Nimrod, great-grandson of Noah, would have its top in the heavens, for the Gate of the God. Their Lord was not happy and scattered his people abroad. So the 5,433 cubits' (some 2,500 m, a cubit is one's forearm length) Tower, built 43 years already, ended there.

One of the key figures of the Hebrew is Moses, also Moshe. A daughter of Pharaoh derived the name from the Egyptian Mū which means "water" and shā "tree", the basket in which the infant Moses floated, came to rest by trees close to Pharaoh's residence. People are familiar with his Decalogue, the *Ten Commandments*, the ten rules that Moses commands all

Israel to obey in the name of God. The contents of the *Ten Commandments* are: 1) All Israel should worship the only God; 2) Do not carve and serve any idol to worship; 3) Do not take the name of God in vain; 4) Keep the Sabbath day and labor in the other six days; 5) Honor your father and mother; 6) Do not kill; 7) Do not commit adultery; 8) Do not steal; 9) Do not bear false witness against others; 10) Do not desire your neighbor's wife, house, field, servants, ox, ass or anything else. Children in the West are familiar with the Mosaic Crosses.

Christianity is by far the most influential religion in the West.

Constantine I of the Roman Empire issued the Edict of Milan and made Christianity legal in 313, and in 381 Theodosius I made Christianity official and outlawed all others. Soon after the fifth century even one of the branches of Christianity called Nestorians reached China. During 1054 Christianity was broken up into the West Church and the East Church.

The *Old Testament* consists of 39 books, the oldest and most important of which are the first five books, called *Pentateuch.* By 1693, the whole of the Bible had been translated into 228 languages. The oldest extant Greek translation of the *Old Testament* is known as the *Septuagint*, simply *LXX.*

When printing was invented in the 1500s, the Latin *Bible* was the first complete work printed. *The Vulgate*, an early Fifth Century version of the *Bible* in Latin, was largely the result of the labors of Jerome. In the 13th century it came to be called versio vulgata, which means "common translation". In 1901, the standard American edition of the Revised Version appeared, known as the *RV*, *The Revised Version* (*or English Revised Version*) *of the King James Version of* 1611.

Jewish greats of all times, known as the "Big 7"—the pillars of Judaism, are Abraham, Isaac and Jacob, Moses and Aaron, David and Solomon. History goes on two 7's generations from Abraham to David, and four 7's generations from David to Christ. In English Abraham means "High Father", "Father of Many Nations". The Arabic for Abraham is Ibrahim.

Man of Peace Solomon's wisdom multiplied talents of gold, hundreds of wives and horses, and genies as well.

Only two books of the *Bible* are about women, one is *Esther*, a Hebrew woman who married a Gentile king of Persian Empire; another is *Ruth* (companion, fellow woman), who once said "Whither thou goest, I will go" to her mother-in-law. What do we do when we are standing at the crossroads of life? When the bottom falls out and we find that our lives need to be rebuilt and redirected? What are the short-term and long-term consequences of our decisions to care for those we love? Ruth made her own choice, not ruthless at all.

With the exception of a few Bedouin nomadic tribes living in the Near East today, the ancient Hebrew culture has disappeared. What happened to this ancient Hebrew thought and culture? Around 800 BCE, a new culture arose to the north. This new culture began to view the world in a way very much different from the Hebrews. This culture was the Greeks. Around200 BCE the Greeks began to move south causing a coming together of the Greek and Hebrew culture. This was a very turbulent time as the two vastly different cultures collided. Over the following 400 years the battle raged until finally the Greek culture won and virtually eliminated all trace of the ancient Hebrew culture. The Greek culture then in turn influenced all the following cultures including the Roman and European cultures, the American culture, and even the modern Hebrew culture in Israel today. 21st Century Americans with a strong Greek thought influence read the Hebrew Bible as if a 21st Century American had written it. In order to understand the ancient Hebrew culture in which the Tanakh was written in, some of the differences between Hebrew and Greek thought must be examined. The word Tanakh is simply another way of saying Old Testament, and it is actually an acronym for the three divisions of the *Hebrew Old Testament*, which are the *Torah* (*Pentateuch* or *Books of Moses*), *Nevi'im* (*Prophets*) and *Ketuvim* (*Writings*).

B. C. E. stands for "Before the common era". It is expected to replace B. C., which means "Before Christ". B. C. and B. C. E. are also identical in value. Most theologians and religious historians believe that the approximate birth date of Yeshua of Nazareth (Jesus) was in the fall, sometime between 4 and 7 B. C. E. CE stands for "Common Era". It is a new term that is eventually expected to replace A. D. A. D. is an acronym for "Anno Domini" in Latin or "the year of the Lord" in English. A. D. refers to the approximate birth year of Yeshua ben Nazareth (a. k. a. Jesus Christ). C. E. and A. D. have the same definition and value. The term "common" simply means that this is the most frequently used calendar system: the Gregorian Calendar. There are many religious calendars in existence, but each of these is normally in use in only a small geographic area of the world—typically by followers of a single religion. Although C. E. and B. C. E. were originally used mainly within theological writings, the terms are gradually receiving greater usage in secular writing, the media, and in the culture generally. This is another way of saying that we/they are being "politically correct".

Greek thought views the world through the mind (abstract thought). Ancient Hebrew thought views the world through the senses (concrete thought). Concrete thought is the expression of concepts and ideas in ways that can be seen, touched, smelled, tasted and/or heard. All five of the senses are used when speaking, hearing, writing, and reading the Hebrew language. An example of this can be found in Psalms 1:3, "He is like a tree planted by streams of water, which yields its fruit in season, and whose leaf does not wither." Abstract thought is the expression of concepts and ideas in ways that can not be seen, touched, smelled, tasted, or heard. Hebrew never uses abstract thought as English does. Examples of abstract thought can be found in Psalms 103:8, "The LORD is compassionate and gracious, slow to anger, abounding in love." Actually words like "anger" in a Hebrew passage are abstract English words that translated the original Hebrew concrete words. The translators often translate this way because the original Hebrew makes no sense when literally translated into English. "Anger", an abstract word, is actually the Hebrew word "awph" which literally means "nose," a concrete word. When one is very angry, he begins to breathe hard and the nostrils begin to flare. A Hebrew sees anger as "the flaring of the nose (nostrils)". If the translator literally translated the above passage "slow to nose", it would make no sense to the English reader.

Greek thought describes objects in relation to its appearance. Hebrew thought describes objects in relation to its function. A deer and an oak are two very different objects. The Hebrew word for both of these objects is "ayil" because the functional descriptions of these two objects are identical to the ancient Hebrews. Therefore, the same Hebrew word is used for both. The Hebraic definition of it is "a strong leader". A deer stag is one of the most powerful animals of the forest and is seen as "a strong leader" among the other animals of the forest. Also the oak tree's wood is very hard compared to other trees such as the pine which is soft and is seen as a "strong leader" among the trees of the forest. Notice the two different translations of the Hebrew word in Psalms 29:9. The NASB and KJV translate it as, "The voice of the LORD makes the deer to calve", while the NIV translates it as, "The voice of the LORD twists the oaks". The literal translation of this verse in Hebrew thought would be, "The voice of the LORD makes the strong leaders turn". When translating the Hebrew into English, the translator must give a Greek description to this word which is why they have two different ways of translating this verse. This same word is also translated as a "ruler" in 2 Kings 24:15, a man who is a strong leader.

Another example of Greek thought would be the following description of a common pencil, "It is yellow and about 8 inches long". A Hebrew description of the pencil would be related to its function such as, "I write words with it." Notice that the Hebrew description uses the verb "write" while the Greek description uses the adjectives "yellow" and "long". Because of Hebrew's form of functional descriptions, verbs are used much more frequently than adjectives.

---

schul：来自德语 shul，复数 shuln，学校

kohen：拉比

Hanukkah：an eight-day Jewish holiday

Code of Hammurabi：汉谟拉比王的法典

Mesopotamia：美索不达米亚（land between two rivers, Tigris（底格里斯河）and Euphrates（幼发拉底河），今中东伊拉克一带）

Mosaic Crosses：马赛克十字架是国外小孩子们的拼图识别十字架的游戏

LXX：七十士译本，传说托勒密（Ptolemy II）为充实亚历山大图书馆组织译的

acronym：首字母缩略词

going-over 复习反馈

multiple-choice Q's

1. 2000 A. D. = ______.

A. MMX　　B. 2000 B. C.　　C. 2000 C. E.

2. A Hebrew sees ______ as the flaring of the nostrils.

A. love　　B. smell　　C. anger

3. *Vulgate* is the ______ version of the *Bible*.

A. Latin　　B. Hebrew　　C. Greek

4. History goes on ______ generations from David to Christ.

A. 14　　B. 28　　C. 42

5. ______ is seen as a "strong leader" by the Jewish people.

A. The oak tree's wood　　B. A deer doe

C. The pine tree's wood

6. The Arabic for ______ is Ibrahim.

A. Abraham　　B. Israelite　　C. Haj

7. Whose name was derived from the Egyptian by a daughter of Pharaoh?

A. Jacob's.　　B. Moses'.　　C. Aaron's.

8. By 1693, the whole of the Bible had been translated in about ______ languages.

A. 100　　B. 200　　C. 400

9. Who of the Roman Empire made Christianity legal?

A. Avignon.　　B. Benedict XVI.C. Constantine I.

essay Q's

10. Tell the difference between Ancient Hebrew thought and Greek thought.

11. What is the Decalogue about?

12. Who is Ruth?

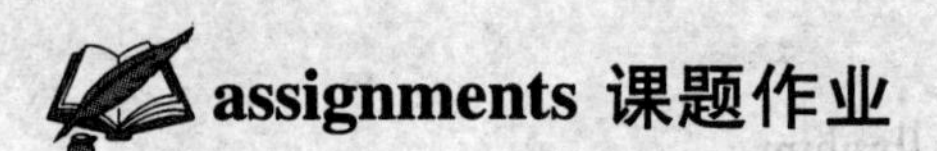

assignments 课题作业

Prepare a brief summary on one of the books of the *Bible*. This assignment may be presented either as a written text or orally in class next time.

extensions 自主拓展

Learn after-class these cultural Q's (questions) for English study. This text is included mainly as entertainment (with A's, reference answers). To how many of them are you able to give a response?

Q's

1. What was the Ark of the Covenant?
2. During whose reign did Jesus of Nazareth live?

3. Whose mother told her daughter to ask her father King Herod for the head of John the Baptist?

4. Many of the expressions found in Jesus' Sermon on the Mount have become well-known idiomatic phrases in the English language. Complete such expressions include the following: (a) hide one's ______ under a bushel, (b) ______ does not know what the right hand is doing, (c) cast ______ before swine, (d) ______ in sheep's clothing.

5. Who asked Christ, "What is truth?" and did not wait for an answer?

6. Was Jesus crucified alone at the place of a skull, Golgotha in Hebrew, on the Sabbath day?

7. Who was the first king of Israel?

8. Who was Queen Jezebel's husband?

9. How much was paid for the betrayal of Jesus Christ?

10. What character in the *Bible* died twice?

11. What judge of Israel was famous for his extraordinary physical strength?

12. The word gospel means "good news", the good news that Jesus brought to the world. Name the four books of *Gospel.*

13. What is the *Pentateuch*?

14. What is the shortest verse in the *Bible*?

15. Daniel was a prophet living in Babylon during the captivity. Who was Shadrach?

16. Solomon had seven hundred wives. Who was the father of Solomon?

17. What are sometimes spoken of as "blood brothers" by savages?

18. Whose sons were Shem, Ham, and Japheth?

19. Complete the following quotation from Burial of the Dead, Com-

mittal in *The Book of Common Prayer*: "We therefore commit his body to the ground; ________, ________, ________; in sure and certain hope of the Resurrection to eternal life, through our Lord Jesus Christ."

20. How long did it take Moses to reach the Promised Land, which roughly corresponds to the present-day Palestine?

21. Who saw the hand-writing on the wall, foretelling the downfall of Babylonia?

22. Members of what religion expose their dead to vultures rather than bury them or, burn them?

23. Where is Mount Ararat, traditionally the landing place of Noah's Ark?

24. Is the same diction employed for "Wilt thou have this woman (/ man) to thy wedded wife (/ husband) ..."?

25. Who was the first Christian martyr?

26. What were the gifts of the Three Wise Men from the east presented unto the Christ Child gently laid in a manger?

27. Name the four main English versions of the *Bible*.

28. Are totem poles idols?

29. How many years of age was Noah when the Flood was upon the earth?

30. Who is Azrael in the Jewish and Mohammedan religions?

31. Where was St. Peter buried?

32. "Make us choose the harder right instead of the easier wrong," is a part of what prayer?

33. What *Bible* is "wicked"?

34. What is Mogen David?

35. Did the ancient Hebrews have images in their temples?

36. What book is the chief hymnal of the Jews?

37. Before and during the Middle Ages, what gemstone was worn by priests as protection from impure thoughts and temptations of the flesh?

A's

1. A sacred chest or box, containing the two stone tablets inscribed with the *Ten Commandments*, the most sacred object of the Temple in Jerusalem, where it was kept in the holy of holies.

2. Of the 1st Roman Emperor Augustus; and of King Herod of Judea. (Christ was actually born in 4 BC in Bethlehem of Judea, NW Jordan, near Jerusalem. However, most of the world measures dates from the birth of Christ.)

3. Salome's.

4. (a) light, (b) the left hand, (c) pearls, (d) a wolf

5. Pontius Pilate, Roman procurator of Judea (26—36 AD), the final authority concerned in the condemnation and execution of Christ. (Pilate wrote a title "This is the King of the Jews", and put it on the cross.)

6. No, two thieves (named Dismas and Gestas) were crucified on either side of Him. (Jesus was 33 years old when he died.)

7. Saul.

8. Ahab, a King of Israel. (Jezebel: a wicked, shameless woman)

9. 30 pieces of silver.

10. Lazarus, a brother of Mary, whom Jesus raised from the dead.

11. Samson. (betrayed by Delilah)

12. (a) Matthew, (b) Mark, (c) Luke, (d) John

13. The first 5 books of the *Old Testament*. (*Genesis*, *Exodus*, *Leviticus*, *Numbers*, *and Deuteronomy*)

14. "Jesus wept." (11:35, the *New Testament*)

15. One of Daniel's companions who was thrown into the fiery furnace of Nebuchadnezzar (a king of Babylonia, conqueror of Jerusalem and

built the Hanging Gardens of Babylon) and came out unharmed.

16. David, 2nd king of Israel. (Abigail: wife of David)

17. Animals, for they believe that animals have souls.

18. Noah's.

19. earth to earth, ashes to ashes, dust to dust

20. 40 years, around 1300 BC. (the Exodus)

21. Belshazzar, a prince of Babylon, son of Nebuchadnezzar.

22. Zoroastrianism

23. In Turkey, near the boarders of Armenia and Iran.

24. No, not all, as "Wilt thou love her, comfort her" and "Wilt thou obey him, serve him".

25. Saint Stephen, died AD 35.

26. gold, frankincense, and myrrh (the Magi: Balthazar, Caspar and Melchior)

27. (a) King James Version, (b) American Revised Version, (c) Douay Bible, and (d) Jewish Version.

28. No, their carved symbols depict family or clan histories and legends.

29. 600. (950 years old when Noah died)

30. Angel of Death, who separates the soul from the body at the moment of death.

31. On the Vatican Hill in Rome. (Simon Peter, one of the 12 apostles, died AD 67)

32. The Cadet's Prayer. (of the West Point)

33. The 1631 edition, for the word "not" had not been printed in the 7th commandment as "Thou shalt not commit adultery."

34. The interlaced, equilateral hexagram, symbol of the Judaism (also shield of David, Star of David, Solomon's Seal)

35. No, because they were forbidden by Mosaic law to make images.

36. Book of Psalms (a collection of 150 psalms)

37. The sapphire (Medieval kings of Europe valued it for rings, believing that it protected them from envy; warriors presented their young wives with sapphire necklaces so they would remain faithful.)

***Numbers*:《民数记》**

Unit Five

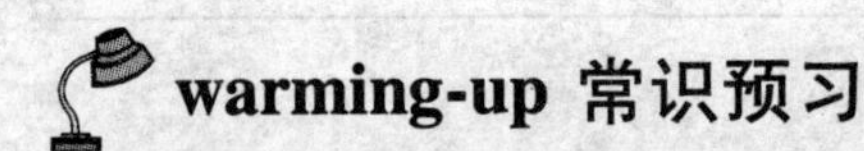

warming-up 常识预习

1. What did the Western Christians do with a return attack against the Moslems?

2. How were people of Western Europe divided under feudalism?

3. From what the western idea of good manners developed?

4. What do you know about the history of castles?

5. Why was Jerusalem important?

6. What is the function of tournaments in the medieval days?

lecturette 专题讲座

The Expansionist Medieval Period

Who destroyed Roman Empire? Scourge of God, Attila of the Huns, Khan of Hunnic Empire who demanded half Western empire as dowry. Between the years 300 to 700 CE the Barbarian Invasions triggered the wandering of the peoples, refugees of the Migration Period, continue well beyond 1000 CE.

In the latter part of the 4th century their tribes swept into Europe from central Asia, robbing and killing a large number of the half civilized Germanic tribes. Many modern European countries owe their origins to events and trends since then, from the fall of the Western Roman Empire. The Middle Ages started, which included the first sustained urbanization of northern and western Europe. In British history, the Middle Ages are often understood to start at the Norman Conquest of 1066 and continue through to about the end of the 15th century (the era between the fall of the Roman Empire and the Norman Conquest is referred to as the Anglo-Saxon period). And the expression "medieval period", often used synonymously with "Middle Ages", is usually used to describe a period of European history when these countries show characteristics of feudal organization.

The Roman Empire reached its greatest territorial extent during the 2nd century. The following two centuries witnessed the slow decline of Roman control over its outlying territories. The Emperor Diocletian split the empire into separately administered eastern and western halves in 285. The division between east and west was encouraged by Constantine, who re-founded the city of Byzantium as the new capital, Constantinople, in 330. Military expenses increased steadily during the 4th century, even as Rome's neighbors became restless and increasingly powerful. Tribes who previously had contact with the Romans as trading partners, rivals, or mercenaries had sought entrance to the empire and access to its wealth throughout the 4th century. Diocletian's reforms had created a strong governmental bureaucracy, reformed taxation, and strengthened the army. These reforms bought the Empire time, but they demanded money. Roman power had been maintained by its well-trained and equipped armies. These armies, however, were a constant drain on the Empire's finances. As warfare became more dependent on heavy cavalry, the infantry-based Roman military started to lose its advantage against its rivals. The defeat in 378 at the Battle of Adrianople, at the hands of mounted Gothic lancers, destroyed much of the Roman army and left the western empire undefended. Without a strong army, the empire was forced to accommodate the large numbers of Germanic tribes who sought refuge within its frontiers.

Known in traditional historiography collectively as the "barbarian invasions", the Migration Period, or the Wandering of the Peoples, this migration was a complicated and gradual process. Some of these "barbarian" tribes rejected the classical culture of Rome, while others admired and aspired to it. In return for land to farm and, in some regions, the right to collect tax revenues for the state, federated tribes provided military support to the empire. Other incursions were small-scale military invasions of tribal groups assembled to gather plunder. The most famous invasion culminated in the sack of Rome by the Visigoths in 410, the first time in almost 800 years that Rome had fallen to an enemy. By the end of the 5th century, Roman institutions were crumbling. As Roman authority disappeared in the west, cities, literacy, trading networks and urban infrastructure declined. Where civic functions and infrastructure were maintained, it was mainly by the Christian Church. The breakdown of Roman society was dramatic. The patchwork of petty rulers was incapable of supporting the depth of civic infrastructure required to maintain libraries, public baths, arenas, and major educational institutions. Any new building was on a far smaller scale than before. The social effects of the fracture of the Roman state were manifold. Cities and merchants lost the economic benefits of safe conditions for trade and manufacture, and intellectual development suffered from the loss of a unified cultural and educational milieu of far-ranging connections.

As it became unsafe to travel or carry goods over any distance, there was a collapse in trade and manufacture for export. The major industries that depended on long-distance trade, such as large-scale pottery manufacture, vanished almost overnight in places like Britain. Between the 5th and 8th centuries, new peoples and powerful individuals filled the political void left by Roman centralized government. Germanic tribes established regional hegemonies within the former boundaries of the Empire, creating divided, decentralized kingdoms like those of the Ostrogoths in Italy, the Visigoths in Hispania, the Franks and Burgundians in Gaul and western Germany, the Angles and the Saxons in Britain, and the Vandals in North Africa.

Alfred the Great, his mother being a Jute, was the ruler of the Anglo-Saxon kingdom of Wessex and contributed greatly to the medieval European culture. Charles the Great, or Charlemagne, embarked in 774 upon a program of systematic expansion that would unify a large portion of Europe. Charlemagne's court in Aachen was the centre of a cultural revival that is sometimes referred to as the Carolingian Renaissance. This period witnessed an increase of literacy, developments in the arts, architecture, and jurisprudence, as well as liturgical and scriptural studies. The English monk Alcuin was invited to Aachen, and brought with him the precise classical Latin education that was available in the monasteries of Northumbria. The return of this Latin proficiency to the kingdom of the Franks is regarded as an important step in the development of Medieval Latin.

Roman landholders beyond the confines of city walls were also vulnerable to extreme changes, and they could not simply pack up their land and move elsewhere. Some were dispossessed and fled to Byzantine regions; others quickly pledged their allegiances to their new rulers. The Muslim conquests of the 7th and 8th centuries of the Persian Empire, Roman Syria, Roman Egypt, Roman North Africa, Visigothic Spain, Sicily and southern Italy eroded the area of the Roman Empire and controlled strategic areas of the Mediterranean Sea. By the end of the 8th century, the former Western Roman Empire was decentralized and overwhelmingly rural. Jerusalem was part of the Muslim possessions won during a rapid military expansion in the 7th century through the Near East, Northern Africa, and

Anatolia (in modern Turkey). Armed pilgrimages intended to liberate Jerusalem from Muslim control. "God will it" (deus vult). Let those who for a long time, have been robbers, now become knights! The first Crusade was preached by Pope Urban II at the Council of Clermont in 1095 in response to a request from the Byzantine emperor Alexios I Komnenos for aid against further advancement. Urban promised indulgence to any Christian who took the Crusader vow and set off for Jerusalem. Sigurd I of Norway (nickname Jorsalafari Jerusalem-farer) was the first European king who went on a crusade. For the first decade, the Crusaders pursued a policy of terror against Muslims and Jews that included mass executions, the throwing of severed heads over besieged cities walls, exhibition and mutilation of naked cadavers, and even cannibalism. The resulting fervor that swept through Europe mobilized tens of thousands of people from all levels of society, and resulted in the capture of Jerusalem in 1099, as well as other regions. The movement found its primary support in the Franks; it is by no coincidence that the Arabs referred to Crusaders generically as Franj. Although they were minorities within this region, the Crusaders tried to consolidate their conquests as a number of Crusader states like the Kingdom of Jerusalem. The Kingdom of Jerusalem made one of the earliest known coats of arms.

During the 12th century and 13th century, there were a series of conflicts between these states and surrounding Islamic ones. Crusades were essentially resupply missions for these embattled kingdoms. Military orders such as the Knights Templar and the Knights Hospitaller were formed to play an integral role in this support. By the end of the Middle Ages, the Christian Crusaders had captured all the Islamic territories in modern Spain, Portugal, and Southern Italy. Meanwhile, Islamic counter-attacks had retaken all the Crusader possessions on the Asian mainland, leaving a de facto boundary between Islam and western Christianity that continued until modern times.

Substantial areas of northern Europe also remained outside Christian influence until the 11th century or later; these areas also became crusading venues. Throughout this period, the Byzantine Empire was in decline, having peaked in influence during the Middle Ages. Beginning with the Battle of Manzikert in 1071, the empire underwent a cycle of decline and renewal, including the sacking of Constantinople by the Fourth Crusade in 1204. After that, Andrew II of Hungary assembled the biggest army in the history of the Crusades, and moved his troops as a leading figure in the Fifth Crusade, reaching Cyprus and later Lebanon, coming back home in 1218. Despite another short upswing following the recapture of Constantinople in 1261, the empire continued to deteriorate. Many people changed their stars during the expansionist Middle Ages, as shown in the movies *A Knight's Tale* and *Robin Hood*, or some even got "promotion" (queening) as in chess. The western Europeans changed many of their old ideas, such as they favored Arabic numerals and drank kahve.

The late Middle Ages were a period initiated by calamities and upheavals. During this time, agriculture was affected by a climate change that has been documented by climate historians, and was felt by contemporaries in the form of periodic famines. The Black Death, a disease that spread among the populace like wildfire, killed as much as a third of the population in the mid-14th century. In some regions, the toll was higher than one half of the population. Even the king Louis I of Hungary was forced to stop his long war against the Kingdom of Naples in 1347, because of the deaths in the Italian region.

---

dowry: money or property brought by a woman to her husband at marriage

cavalry: troops trained to fight on horseback

infantry: soldiers who fight on foot

mounted: riding on a horse

incursion: PM a sudden attack into an area that belongs to other people

plunder: things that have been stolen during a violent attack, especially during a war

culminate: end, especially to reach a final or climactic stage

sack: go through (a place) destroying or stealing things and attacking people

patchwork: something that is made up of a lot of different things 拼凑的东西,混杂物

petty: inferior in rank or status; not important and not worth giving attention to

manifold: many and of different kinds

milieu: the environmental condition

hegemony: a situation in which one state or country controls others

embark upon: to start something, especially something new, difficult, or exciting

jurisprudence: the science or study of law

liturgical: 礼拜式的

scriptural: 圣经的,依据圣经的

cadaver: the dead body of a human being

cannibalism: the practice of eating the flesh of your own kind

fervor: very strong belief or feeling

de facto: in reality or fact

promotion: (国际象棋)兵升变,变后

kahve：咖啡，土耳其的原始饮料，在意大利受洗过

going-over 复习反馈

multiple-choice Q's

1. What characteristics did the medieval period show?

A. Roman control　　B. Viking power

C. feudal organization

2. An instance that the Western Europeans changed one of their old ideas is that ______.

A. they changed their stars　　B. they drank tea

C. they favored Arabic numerals

3. Today the boundary between Islam and western Christianity was formerly shaped by ______.

A. Sigurd I of Norway　　B. the Byzantine Empire

C. the Crusaders

4. Charlemagne's cultural revival is sometimes referred to as ______.

A. the Carolingian Renaissance　　B. the Wandering of the Peoples

C. the Liberation of Jerusalem from Muslim control

5. Who assembled the biggest army in the history of the Crusades?

A. Andrew II of Hungary.　　B. Louis I of Hungary.

C. Alexios I Komnenos.

6. When was the first Crusade preached by Pope Urban II at the Council of Clermont?

A. In 1071.　　B. In 1095.　　C. In 1099.

7. By the end of the Middle Ages, the Christian Crusaders had captured all the Islamic territories in modern Spain, Portugal, and ______.

A. Southern Italy　　B. Northern Africa

C. Near East

8. What Kingdom made one of the earliest known coats of arms?

A. Kingdom of Jerusalem. B. Kingdom of the Franks.

C. Kingdom of Naples.

9. Where were the kingdoms of the Ostrogoths?

A. In Germany. B. In Italy. C. In Gaul.

essay Q's

10. What is the significance of "the Barbarian Invasions"?

11. Do you know 1066 and all that?

12. Why is the medieval period sometimes called expansionist Middle Ages?

assignments 课题作业

Prepare a brief summary on the cultural development of the medieval period. This assignment may be presented either as a written text or orally in class next time.

Appreciate after-class the action-adventure movie "A Knight's Tale". This text is included mainly as entertainment. What is your understanding of the code of chivalry?

A Knight's Tale is a 2001 American action-adventure film directed, produced, and written by Brian Helgeland. The film takes its title from Chaucer's "The Knight's Tale" in his *Canterbury Tales*.

Set in late Medieval Europe in the 1370s, the story begins with the protagonists and squires, William, Roland and Wat, discovering their master, Sir Ector, dead of bowel problems in the middle of a jousting tournament. He was ahead "three lances to none" and merely had to finish the final round to win the tournament and be awarded the money that was to buy food for them all. While Wat and Roland resign themselves to destitution now that they no longer have Sir Ector's employment and protection, William Thatcher takes the armor, and more importantly the helm, from Ector's body and poses as the noble to finish the match. William's inexperience is evident, as he disappointingly receives a lance blow to the face mask, but regardless wins the tournament (and the money) due to Ector's previous lead. This gives William the idea that, with proper training, he and his companions could make a living in jousting.

Way to his first tournament in Rouen, William and his friends come upon Geoffrey Chaucer, "trudging" down a road with no clothes or money. William persuades the writer to fake his patents of nobility, as it is illegal for peasants to joust, and joins the jousting circuit under the pseudonym of

"Sir Ulrich von Liechtenstein" from Gelderland. Chaucer is then discovered to have a terrible gambling problem, which William saves him from by paying his debts with his tournament winnings, and therefore gains Geoffrey's true loyalty (and services as a herald at the tournaments). Helped by Chaucer, Wat and Roland, he begins to win match after match. When his armor—still the same suit taken from Sir Ector—becomes loose and damaged, he gains an addition to his fellowship, Kate the Farrier, who makes him revolutionary new armor and decides to travel with them. William soon meets and falls in love with a noble lady, Jocelyn, who has already been noticed by the evil yet powerful Count Adhemar. A rivalry begins between the two of them for the affection of Jocelyn and the accolades of the tournaments, and Adhemar defeats William in his first tournament.

In the following tournament, they are both assigned to tilt against Prince Edward, who has entered under the name "Sir Thomas Colville", hoping he will get a rare chance to compete if his opponents do not know his identity as the Prince of Wales. Adhemar learns his identity and withdraws at the last minute, not willing to take the risk. When William's turn comes, however, his competitiveness overcomes the pressure to withdraw, and he jousts with Edward (to Edward's surprise and pleasure) and wins the tournament, along with Edward's respect. Following this good omen, Will's companions, Wat, Roland, Kate and Geoff, gamble all of their share of the money that William will win the French tournament in Paris. Coincidentally, and simultaneously, Jocelyn tells William that he must lose the tournament to prove his love to her. After he openly accepts defeat after defeat, she changes her mind; that is, he must now win to prove his love. He does win the tournament, which is followed by a romantic scene.

The group travels to London for the World Championship, and an important flashback to William's childhood is shown. His father, wanting the best for his son, reluctantly gives him over for squire services to Sir Ector, so that someday, he can realize his dream of becoming a knight and "change his stars" to live a better life than his father. Returning to the present—and to London for the first time since childhood—William, assuming that his father has long since died, visits his old neighborhood and inquires of a young local girl whether or not she remembers his father. She informs him that he is in fact still alive and well, albeit blind. William visits his father, concealing himself at first using his alias Ulrich, until he tells his father that he has a message from his son William—that he has changed his stars after all. His father, overcome with joyous emotion, realizes it is actually his son, and they embrace and spend hours catching up.

Although everything appears well, Adhemar has returned from fighting in the Battle of Poitiers and discovers William's humble origins. He alerts the authorities to the secret. William's friends beg him to flee, including Jocelyn, who promises to give up her privileged life and run away with him, but he refuses to run and is arrested. Adhemar visits him in prison and gloats that he will marry Jocelyn while beating the defenseless William. When William is moved to the stocks, his companions all stand with him to defend him from the crowd, which grows increasingly hostile until Prince Edward emerges from the mob. He orders William to be released, telling the crowd that his historians have discovered that William is descendant from an "ancient royal line" and that he is entitled to a knighthood after all. The newly dubbed "Sir William" goes on to resume his place in the tournament and compete against Adhemar.

With Jocelyn and William's father in attendance, Adhemar cheats with an illegal lance with a sharp point on the tip, which stabs into William's shoulder during the first round. William, unable to grip his lance or breathe properly due to his injury, has his armor removed and his lance strapped to his arm and competes in the final round wearing only ordinary clothing. The two adversaries charge for the final bout, with William's life in the balance. He shouts his finally accepted true name, "WILLIAM," and knocks Adhemar from his horse, winning the tournament. Chaucer remarks that he should write this whole story down, a reference to "The Knight's Tale" of the *Canterbury Tales*. Jocelyn runs out ecstatically to meet William and they embrace in a long kiss.

---

protagonist: main character

squire: a young man in the Middle Ages who learned how to be a knight by serving one 侍从

destitution: the state of having no money, food, a home or possessions

take the helm: to start being in charge of something such as a business or organization

herald: a person who carried important messages and made announcements in the past

accolade: praise and approval

albeit: although

catch up: to learn or discuss the latest news

gloat: to feel or express great pleasure or satisfaction because of your own success or good luck, or someone else's failure or bad luck

adversary: opponent

in the balance: in a situation where you cannot yet know whether the result will be bad or good

ecstatic: feeling extremely happy and excited

Unit Six

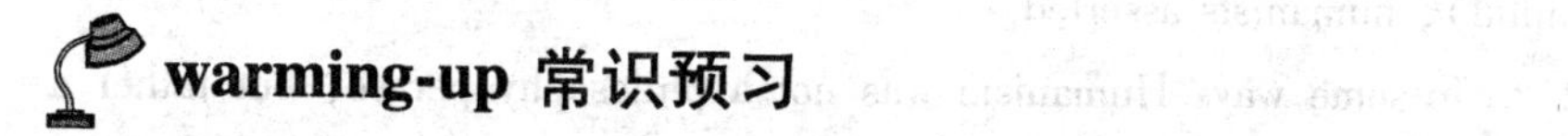

warming-up 常识预习

1. What is the essence of the Renaissance?

2. Where did Renaissance start with the flowering of paintings, sculpture and architecture?

3. Among Leonardo da Vinci's major works, which is the most famous of religious pictures?

4. What style of art did Michelangelo create?

5. Who is looked up as the father of modern poetry?

6. What made Italy the birthplace of the Renaissance?

lecturette 专题讲座

Bridge Between the Middle Ages and the Modern Era

Renaissance was a cultural movement that spanned roughly the 14th to the 17th century, beginning in Florence in the Late Middle Ages and later spreading to the rest of Europe. As a cultural movement, it encompassed a resurgence of learning based on classical sources, the development of linear perspective in painting, and gradual but widespread educational reform. Traditionally, this intellectual transformation has resulted in the Renaissance being viewed as a bridge between the Middle Ages and the Modern

Era. Although the Renaissance saw revolutions in many intellectual pursuits, as well as social and political upheaval, it is perhaps best known for its artistic developments and the contributions of such polymaths as Leonardo da Vinci and Michelangelo, who inspired the term *Renaissance man*, "the genius of man" (the unique and extraordinary ability of the human mind), humanists asserted.

In some ways Humanism was not a philosophy per se, but rather a method of learning. In contrast to the medieval scholastic mode, which focused on resolving contradictions between authors, humanists would study ancient texts in the original, and appraise them through a combination of reasoning and empirical evidence. Humanist education was based on the program of Studia Humanitatis, that being the study of five humanities: poetry, grammar, history, moral philosophy and rhetoric. Although historians have sometimes struggled to define humanism precisely, most have settled on a middle of the road definition "the movement to recover, interpret, and assimilate the language, literature, learning and values of ancient Greece and Rome".

One of the distinguishing features of Renaissance art was its development of highly realistic linear perspective. Giotto (1267—1337) is credited with first treating a painting as a window into space, but it was not until the demonstrations of architect Brunelleschi (1377—1446) that perspective was formalized as an artistic technique. The development of perspective was part of a wider trend towards realism in the arts. To that end, painters also developed other techniques, studying light, shadow, and, famously in the case of Leonardo da Vinci, human anatomy. Underlying these changes in artistic method, was a renewed desire to depict the beauty of nature, and to unravel the axioms of aesthetics, with the works of Leonardo, Michelangelo and Raphael representing artistic pinnacles that were to be much imitated by other artists. Other notable artists include Botticelli, working for the Medici in Florence, Donatello another Florentine and Titian in Venice, among others. In architecture, Brunelleschi was foremost in studying the remains of ancient classical buildings, and with rediscovered knowledge from the 1st-century writer Vitruvius and the flourishing discipline of mathematics, formulated the Renaissance style which emulated and improved on classical forms. Brunelleschi's major feat of engineering was the building of the dome of Florence Cathedral. The first building to demonstrate this is claimed to be the church of St. Andrew built by Alberti in Mantua. The outstanding architectural work of the High Renaissance was the rebuilding of St. Peter's Basilica, combining the skills of Bramante, Michelangelo, Raphael, Sangallo and Maderno. The five types of Roman columns are used: Tuscan, Doric, Ionic, Corinthian and Composite. These can either be structural, supporting an arcade or architrave, or purely decorative, set against a wall in the form of pilasters. During the Renaissance, architects aimed to use columns, pilasters, and entablatures as an integrated system. One of the first buildings to use pilasters as an integrated system was in the Old Sacristy (1421—1440) by Brunelleschi. Arches, semi-circular or (in the Mannerist style) segmental, are often used in arcades, supported on piers or columns with capitals. There may be a section of entablature between the capital and the springing of the arch. Alberti was one of the first to use the arch on a monumental. Renaissance vaults do not have ribs. They are semi-circular or segmental and on a square plan, unlike the Gothic vault which is frequently rectangular.

The upheavals occurring in the arts and humanities were mirrored by a dynamic period of change in the sciences. Some have seen this flurry of activity as a scientific revolution, heralding the beginning of the modern age. Others have seen it merely as an acceleration of a continuous process stretching from the ancient world to the present day. Regardless, there is general agreement that the Renaissance saw significant changes in the way the universe was viewed and the methods with which philosophers sought to explain natural phenomena.

Science and art were very much intermingled in the early Renaissance, with artists such as Leonardo da Vinci making observational drawings of anatomy and nature. Leonardo was a much greater scientist than previously thought, and not just an inventor. In science theory and in conducting actual science practice, Leonardo was innovative. He set up controlled experiments in water flow, medical dissection, and systematic study of movement and aerodynamics; he devised principles of research method that classify him as "father of modern science". Leonardo's science is more in tune with holistic non-mechanistic and non-reductive approaches to science which are becoming popular today. Perhaps the most significant development of the era was not a specific discovery, but rather a process for discovery, the scientific method. This revolutionary new way of learning about the world focused on empirical evidence, the importance of mathematics, and discarding the Aristotelian final cause in favor of a mechanical philosophy. Early and influential proponents of these ideas included Copernicus and Galileo. The Copernican revolution really is the Galilean-Cartesian (René Descartes) revolution, on account of the nature of the courage and depth of change their work brought about. The new scientific method led to great contributions in the fields of astronomy, physics, biology, and anatomy.

The new ideals of humanism, although more secular in some aspects, developed against a Christian backdrop, especially in the Northern Renaissance. Indeed, much (if not most) of the new art was commissioned by or in dedication to the Church. However, the Renaissance had a profound effect on contemporary theology, particularly in the way people perceived the relationship between man and God. Many of the period's foremost theologians were followers of the humanist method, including Erasmus, Zwingli, Thomas More, Martin Luther, and John Calvin.

The Renaissance began in times of religious turmoil. The late Middle Ages saw a period of political intrigue surrounding the Papacy, culminating in the Western Schism, in which three men simultaneously claimed to be true Bishop of Rome. While the schism was resolved by the Council of Constance, the 15th century saw a resulting reform movement know as Conciliarism, which sought to limit the pope's power. Although the papacy eventually emerged supreme in ecclesiastical matters by the Fifth Council of the Lateran, it was dogged by continued accusations of corruption, most famously in the person of Pope Alexander VI, who was accused variously of simony, nepotism and fathering four illegitimate children whilst Pope, whom he married off to gain more power. Churchmen such as Erasmus and Luther proposed reform to the Church, often based on humanist textual criticism of the New Testament. Indeed, it was Luther who in October 1517 published the 95 *Theses*, challenging papal authority and criticizing its perceived corruption, particularly with regard to its sale of indulgences. The 95 *Theses* led to the Reformation, a break with the Roman Catholic Church that previously claimed hegemony in Western Europe. Humanism and the Renaissance therefore played a direct role in sparking the Reformation, as well as in many other contemporaneous religious debates and conflicts.

By the 15th century, writers, artists and architects in Italy were well aware of the transformations that were taking place and were using phrases like modi antichi (in the antique manner) or alle romana et alla antica (in the manner of the Romans and the ancients) to describe their work. The term la rinascita first appeared, however, in its broad sense in Giorgio Vasari's *The Lives of the Artists*1550. Vasari divides the age into three phases: the first phase contains Cimabue, Giotto, and Arnolfo di Cambio; the second phase contains Masaccio, Brunelleschi, and Donatello; the third centers on Leonardo da Vinci and culminates with Michelangelo. It was not just the growing awareness of classical antiquity that drove this development, according to Vasari, but also the growing desire to study and imitate nature. In the 15th century, the Renaissance spread with great speed from its birthplace in Florence, first to the rest of Italy, and soon to the rest of Europe. The invention of the printing press allowed the rapid transmission of these new ideas. As it spread, its ideas diversified and changed, being adapted to local culture. In the 20th century, scholars began to break the Renaissance into regional and national movements.

In 1495 the Italian Renaissance arrived in France, imported by King Charles VIII after his invasion of Italy. A factor that promoted the spread of secularism was the Church's inability to offer assistance against the Black Death. Francis I imported Italian art and artists, including Leonardo da Vinci, and built ornate palaces at great expense. Writers such as François Rabelais, Pierre de Ronsard, Joachim du Bellay and Michel de Montaigne, painters such as Jean Clouet and musicians such as Jean Mouton also borrowed from the spirit of the Italian Renaissance. In 1533, a fourteen-year old Caterina de' Medici, born in Florence to Lorenzo II de' Medici and Madeleine de la Tour d'Auvergne married Henry, second son of King Francis I and Queen Claude. Though she became famous and infamous for her role in France's religious wars, she made a direct contribution in bringing arts, sciences and music (including the origins of ballet) to the French court from her native Florence.

---

resurgence: revival, reappearance

polymath: a person of great and varied learning

per se: by or of itself

pinnacle: the most successful, powerful, exciting etc. part of something

column: a tall solid upright stone post used to support a building or as a decoration

pilaster: a flat square column attached to the wall of a building for decoration

entablature: the structure consisting of the part of a classical temple above the columns between a capital and the roof

vault: a roof or ceiling that consists of several arches that are joined together, esp. in a church

secular: not having any connection with religion

the Papacy: the position and authority of the Pope

schism: a split or division

ecclesiastical: relating to the Christian church or its priests

simony: 僧职买卖(罪)

nepotism: 裙带关系,任人唯亲

papal: relating to the Pope

indulgence: a promise of freedom from punishment by God, sold by priests in the Middle Ages

secularism: a doctrine that rejects religion and religious considerations

Petrarch: 彼德拉克(1304—1374),father of modern poetry

Donatello: 多纳太罗(1386—1466),骑马雕像(equestrian)的始祖

Erasmus: 伊拉斯谟(1466—1536),撰有《伊拉斯谟格言》(*The Adagia of Erasmus*)

Flanders: 法兰德斯,荷兰和比利时一带(北部脱离西班牙独立,

成为今日的荷兰）

going-over 复习反馈

multiple-choice Q's

1. Which of the following humanities was NOT studied for humanist education?

A. Grammar.　B. Math.　C. Rhetoric.

2. Who first treated a painting as a window into space?

A. Titian.　B. Giotto.　C. Raphael.

3. Which notable artist worked for the Medici?

A. Donatello.　B. Titian.　C. Raphael.

4. Where did the cultural movement Renaissance begin?

A. In Troy.　B. In Rome.　C. In Florence.

5. Who inspired the term Renaissance man?

A. Petrarch.　B. Erasmus.　C. Michelangelo.

6. Which of the following is NOT a French writer?

A. Cervantes.　B. Montaigne.　C. Rabelais.

7. Which of the following was NOT a follower of the humanist method?

A. Erasmus.　B. Flemish.　C. Thomas More.

8. Who imported the Italian Renaissance into France?

A. King Francis VIII.　B. King Henry VIII.

C. King Charles VIII.

9. Of what was Pope Alexander VI accused?

A. Nepotism.

B. Fathering five illegitimate children.

C. Poach.

essay Q's

10. What made Italy the birthplace of the Renaissance?

11. In what way is Leonardo da Vinci known as father of modern science?

12. Are there any differences between the big 3 protestants—the Lutheran, Calvinist, and Anglican Church?

assignments 课题作业

Prepare a brief summary on the cultural movement Renaissance. This assignment may be presented either as a written text or orally in class next time.

extensions 自主拓展

Learn after-class the adages compiled by Erasmus. This text is included mainly as entertainment. What are their Chinese equivalents?

Erasmus of Rotterdam (1466—1536) was a Dutch Renaissance humanist and a Catholic priest and theologian. Erasmus was a classical scholar who wrote in a pure Latin style and enjoyed the sobriquet Prince of the Humanists. He has been called "the crowning glory of the Christian humanists". Using humanist techniques for working on texts, he prepared important new Latin and Greek editions of the New Testament. These raised questions that would be influential in the Protestant Reformation and Catholic Counter-Reformation. Erasmus lived through the Reformation period and he consistently criticized some contemporary popular Christian beliefs. In relation to clerical abuses in the Church, Erasmus remained committed to reforming the Church from within. He also held to Catholic doctrines such as that of free will, which some Protestant Reformers rejected in favor of the doctrine of predestination. His middle road disappointed and even angered many Protestants, such as Martin Luther, as well as conservative Catholics. He died in Basel in 1536 and was buried in the formerly Catholic cathedral there, recently converted to a Reformed church.

Although associated closely with Rotterdam, Erasmus lived there for only four years, never to return. Information on his family and early life comes mainly from vague references in his writings. His parents almost certainly were not legally married. His father, named Roger Gerard, later became a priest and afterwards curate in Gouda. Little is known of his mother other than that her name was Margaret and she was the daughter of a physician. Although he was born out of wedlock, Erasmus was cared for by his parents until their early deaths from the plague in 1483. He was then given the very best education available to a young man of his day, in a series of monastic or semi-monastic schools, most notably a school run by the Brethren of the Common Life (inspired by Geert Groote) where he gleaned the importance of a personal relationship with God but eschewed the harsh rules and strict methods of the religious brothers and educators. While at the Augustinian monastery Steyn near Gouda around 1487, young Erasmus wrote a series of passionate letters to a fellow monk, Servatius Rogerus, whom he called "half my soul", writing, "I have wooed you both unhappily and relentlessly"; Whether this is evidence for simply male-to-male friendship is unclear; nevertheless this correspondence contrasts sharply with the generally detached and much more restrained attitude he showed in his later life. Of similar interest was the sudden dismissal by the guardian of Thomas Grey, a student Erasmus tutored in Paris which could be taken as grounds of an illicit affair. However, no personal denunciation was made of Erasmus during his lifetime. He took pains to condemn sodomy in his works, and instead praised sexual desire in the context of marriage between men and women.

Erasmus compiled an annotated collection of Greek and Latin adages called *Adagia*, which is one of the most monumental collections of adagia ever assembled. The collection is the fruit of Erasmus' vast reading in classical literature; he expanded it occasionally throughout his career, and the book did not attain its final form until close to his death. The first edition, titled *Collecteana Adagiorum*, was published in Paris in 1500, in a slim quarto of around eight hundred proverbs. By the end of his time in Italy, Erasmus had expanded the collection to over three thousand items, many accompanied by explanatory notes that are often, in fact, brief essays on political and moral topics. He had also changed the title to *Adagiorum Chiliades* (the thousand proverbs). This was the title it retained in all subsequent editions. By his death, Erasmus had compiled 4,658 adages in his collection. Many have become commonplace in our everyday language, and we owe our use of them to Erasmus. Among these are:

Make haste slowly / One step at a time / To be in the same boat / To lead one by the nose

A rare bird / Even a child can see it / To walk on tiptoe / One to one / Out of tune / A point in time

To have one foot in Charon's boat (To have one foot in the grave) / To call a spade a spade

I gave as bad as I got (I gave as good as I got) / Hatched from the same egg / A living corpse

Up to both ears (Up to his eyeballs) / As though in a mirror / Think before you start

What's done cannot be undone / Many parasangs ahead (Miles ahead) / To cut to the quick

We cannot all do everything / Many hands make light work / Where there's life, there's hope

Time reveals all things / Golden handcuffs / Crocodile tears / To show the middle finger

You have touched the issue with a needle-point (To have nailed it) / To walk the tightrope

Time tempers grief (Time heals all wounds) / With a fair wind / To dangle the bait

To swallow the hook / The bowels of the earth / From heaven to earth / To weigh anchor

The dog is worthy of his dinner / To grind one's teeth / Nowhere near the mark

Complete the circle / In the land of the blind, the one-eyed man is king / A cough for a fart

No sooner said than done / There's many a slip 'twixt cup and lip /

A necessary evil

Neither with bad things nor without them (Women can't live with 'em, can't live without 'em)

Between a stone and a shrine (Between a rock and a hard place) / Dog in the manger

Like teaching an old man a new language (Can't teach an old dog new tricks) / To sleep on it

To squeeze water out of a stone / To leave no stone unturned / The grass is greener over the fence

Let the cobbler stick to his last (Stick to your knitting) / God helps those who help themselves

The cart before the horse / One swallow doesn't make a summer / His heart was in his boots

To break the ice / Ship-shape / To die of laughing / Like father, like son / To show one's heels

To have an iron in the fire / To look a gift horse in the mouth / Neither fish nor flesh

Not worth a snap of the fingers / He blows his own trumpet

---

sobriquet: nickname

curate: a priest of the lowest rank, whose job is to help the priest who is in charge of an area

born out of wedlock: 非婚生的,私生的

eschew: to deliberately avoid doing or using something

denunciation: a public statement in which you criticize someone or something

annotate: to add a short explanation or opinion to a text or drawing

adage: proverb

quarto: 四开

Unit Seven

warming-up 常识预习

1. What's Newton's contribution to the science?

2. Who first discovered four moons of Jupiter?

3. What event was called the Glorious Revolution?

4. How did Bacon attack on the unscientific thinking?

5. Why Leibniz' interest in China was of great significance for computing science today?

6. Which country in the mid-17th century was most powerful in Europe?

lecturette 专题讲座

Issues of the 17th Century Europe and Their Influence

The 17th century is probably the most important century in the making of the modern world. It was during the 1600s that Galileo and Newton founded modern science; that Descartes began modern philosophy; that Hugo Grotius initiated international law; that Thomas Hobbes and John Locke started modern political theory. In the same century strong centralized European states entered into worldwide international competition for wealth and power, accelerating the pace of colonization in America and Asia. The Dutch, French, Spanish, Portuguese, English, and others, all struggled to maintain and extend colonies and trading-posts in distant corners of the globe, with profound and permanent consequences for the whole world. They also fought one another in Europe, where warfare grew increasingly complex and expensive. To gain an edge against other powers in war, European governments invested in research in military technology, and the seventeenth century was consequently an age of military revolution, enabling Europeans from then on to defeat most non-European peoples relatively easily in battle.

European religious divisions occurred at the opening of the 17th century, the divisions that led to assassinations and to widespread warfare, especially in the Thirty Years War of 1618—1648. This war devastated much of Germany, and for a while made Sweden a great power. It also profoundly affected France, Spain and the Netherlands. In France, Cardinal Richelieu and Jules Mazarin strengthened and centralized state power, though at times their policies came perilously close to disaster. In Spain, disaster struck, and the Spaniards lost their long war with the Dutch, who formed a prosperous independent republic. Spain also lost control of Portugal, and for a while it seemed that Catalonia too would break free from Spanish control.

Spain declined but France rose to become the greatest power in Europe. In the second half of the 17th century Louis XIV increased royal power at home and French power abroad, but at a very high cost in lives and cash. The France of Louis XIV threatened to dominate Europe, and to oppose him other powers laid aside their religious differences (which were becoming less important in the increasingly secularized and scientific atmosphere of the late 1600s) and joined forces against France. By the end of the century two powers in particular were rivaling France, namely Holland and England. Both benefited from the shift of Europe's economic center of gravity from the Mediterranean to the Atlantic. In both, agricultural and commercial changes were taking place which would soon pave the way for the Industrial Revolution.

As for cultural movement the 17th century falls into the early modern period of Europe and was characterized by Baroque art. This main style of art flourished in Italy, and then spread to Spain, Portugal, France and other parts of Europe. The term "baroque" was first applied to the architecture of the period, with its proliferation of ornament, and then extended to its elaborate painting and music. It was characterized by dramatic intensity and sentimental appeal with a lot of emphasis on light and color. Rubens helped to spread the Baroque style to North Europe.

These were the great social issues of the age, and they had a great influence on the way people lived and dressed. The clothing worn by Europeans during the 17th century was influenced by fashion trends—rapid changes in style influenced by trendsetters—as never before. During the course of the century garments went from restrictive to comfortable and back to restrictive again, and excessive ornament was both stripped away and added back to clothing for both men and women.

A baldric was a broad belt that was strapped over the shoulder; it extended diagonally across the chest, usually from the right shoulder to the left hip. Breeches remained the most common form of legwear for men. Women wore bustles underneath the backs of their skirts for several centuries beginning in the sixteenth. Bustles consisted of cushions, pads, and frames made of wire and wood, that were tied around the waist or directly attached to a woman's skirts. Neckwear was an important component of dress for both men and women in the 16th and 17th centuries, and they devised many ways to decorate the neck. Most popular were the ruff, a stiffly frilled collar that encircled the neck, and the whisk, a wide fanned collar around the back of the neck. The primary garment worn by women of all social classes was the gown, consisting of a close-fitting bodice with attached decorative sleeves and full skirts. A long coat worn over a shirt and vest, the justaucorps was one of the most common overgarments worn by men during the 17th century. Petticoats were full skirts that women wore beneath another skirt beginning in the 15th century. There were several reasons for wearing petticoats. The stomacher was an essential part of women's gowns, from about 1570 to 1770. In its most basic form it was a long V-or U-shaped panel that decorated the front of a woman's bodice, extending from her neckline down to her waist. The waistcoat has been one of the standard pieces of formal dress in the West since the late sixteenth century, and it has gone through several changes over time. From the 16th through the 18th centuries, men's waistcoats were long-sleeved garments worn as middle layers of clothing, over a shirt but underneath a topcoat or justaucorps. Related to the standing collar and the ruff, the whisk was an especially stiff and ornate neck decoration worn during the first decades. Like many fashion trends of this period, the whisk originated in Spain, and evolved from the golilla. A well-groomed head was important for both men and women during the seventeenth century. At the beginning of the century fashionable men wore their natural hair quite long with lovelocks, or extra long strands of hair, dangling over their left shoulder. In 1680 the fontange became the most fashionable women's hairstyle and remained popular until the early 18th century. The style was created by the Duchesse de Fontanges, the mistress of the French king Louis XIV, when the hairstyle she was wearing at the time was ruined while out hunting. Originating in Paris, France, the hurly-burly, also known as hurluberlu, became a fashionable hairstyle for women during the Baroque period of the seventeenth century, during which time people favored extravagant fashions. The hurly-burly consisted of shoulder length or shorter curls falling in ringlets from a dramatic center part to frame a woman's face. Lovelocks were a small lock of hair that cascaded from the crown of the head down over the left shoulder. Lovelocks were longer than the rest of the hair and were treated as special features. Worn with one point forward, the tricorne hat emerged as the most fashionable hat for men for most of the 18th century. Courtesy of the Library of Congress. Wigs became a necessity for French courtiers (officers and advisers) in 1643 when 16-year-old Louis XIV ascended the throne sporting long curly hair. For all who could not grow their own, long flowing locks were created with wigs. While the 16th century was an age of excess in ornamentation, the 17th century is often thought of as an age of elegance, with greater care for the manner of display than for its abundance. Nowhere is this contrast more evident than in the use of jewelry.

The cane emerged as an important fashion accessory for men during the 17th century and was every bit as important in a carefully dressed man's wardrobe as gloves and a hat. Although people had carried rough walking sticks or simple canes for centuries, it was during this period that these sticks became carefully crafted items carried by every gentleman. The cravat, introduced in the mid-17th century, is the ancestor of the modern necktie. A long strip of cloth wrapped loosely around the neck, the cravat was one of several items to replace the stiff ruffs worn around the neck in the 16th and early 17th centuries.

One of the most unique jewelry innovations of the 17th century was the earstring. Both men and women wore earrings during this period, and many added an earstring as well. Perhaps the most important accessory for wealthy women was the folding fan. Made of fine materials such as silk or decorated paper, stretched between handles of ivory, carved wood, or even fine gold, and studded with jewels, fans were an item used to display the user's wealth and distinction. Often considered one of the strangest accessories, masks had both practical and decorative uses among European women. Masks were first worn during the 16th century to provide protection from the sun and other elements while women were outside or riding horses, thus preserving the pale complexion that was in fashion. Heating the castles and great halls of wealthy people in the 17th century was not easy, especially in the cooler countries in the north, such as England and Scotland. Stone walls and fireplaces in nearly every room could not keep rooms warm enough when the days grew cold. While the placing of false beauty marks, or patches, on the face began in ancient Rome around the first century C. E., it became a widespread fad across Europe from the late 1500s through the 1600s. A dark mole that occurs naturally on the face is sometimes called a beauty mark. People took great care covering their feet. Fashionable footwear changed shape during the century, and middle-class and wealthy people eagerly purchased the new shoe styles in order to remain in fashion. One of the most important fashion trendsetters during the 17th century was the cavalier, or military horseman. Along with his confident swagger, his costume came to mark a certain male style during the century. Height was a central feature of 17th century fashion. People accentuated their height with tall hairstyles, long flowing gowns, long straight jackets, and high-heeled shoes. Ice skating became a popular winter activity. The idea of gliding across ice had intrigued people for thousands of years, and ice skates had evolved from extremely primitive foot coverings into sleekly designed footwear. When shoes with fastenings replaced slip-on styles at the end of the 16th century, shoe decoration started to become important. These new shoe styles featured latchets, or straps, that crossed over the top of the foot near the ankle.

Newton：牛顿爵士(1643—1727)

Galileo：伽利略(1564—1642)

Rubens：鲁本斯(1577—1640，佛兰德斯画家，巴洛克画派早期的代表人物)

trendsetter：someone who starts a new fashion or makes it popular

breeches：short trousers that fasten just below the knees

bustle：a frame worn by women in the past to hold out the back of their skirts

golilla：a stiff linen collar projecting at right angles from the neck

lovelock：伊丽莎白女皇及詹姆斯一世时流行的上层社会中男子在耳边用丝带等结扎的垂发

cravat：a wide piece of loosely folded material that men wear around their necks

fad：something that people like or do for a short time，or that is fashionable for a short time

going-over 复习反馈

multiple-choice Q's

1. The 17th century saw ______ rose to become the greatest power in Europe.

A. Spain B. France C. Holland

2. What is the main style of art for the 17th Century Europe?

A. Romantic. B. Baroque. C. Realistic.

3. ______ is the greatest name in physics in the 17th century.

A. Galileo B. Louis XIV C. Descartes

4. Who began modern philosophy?

A. Galileo. B. Louis XIV. C. Descartes.

5. ______ benefited from the shift of Europe's economic center from the Mediterranean to the Atlantic by the end of the 17th century.

A. England B. Portugal C. Austria

6. Neckwear was an important component of dress for both men and women in the 17th century.

A. Not mentioned B. False

C. True

7. ______ was a central feature of 17th-century fashion.

A. Height B. Fancy dress C. Being formal

8. A fontange is the name of a(n) ______ popular in the late seventeenth century in France.

A. earstring B. hairstyle C. wardrobe

9. What was the primary garment worn by women of all social classes of the 17th century?

A. The hurly-burly. B. The mask.

C. The gown.

essay Q's

10. How was the clothing worn by Europeans during the 17th century influenced by fashion trends?

11. What caused the seventeenth century to be an age of military revolution?

12. Why is the 17th century probably the most important century in the making of the modern world?

assignments 课题作业

Prepare a brief summary on the warfare of the 17th century. This assignment may be presented either as a written text or orally in class next time.

extensions 自主拓展

Learn after-class the essay "Of Studies" by the first major English essayist Francis Bacon. This text is included mainly as entertainment. What other famous lines have you learnt from Bacon?

Francis Bacon, 1st Viscount St Alban, KC (1561—1626) was an English philosopher, statesman, scientist, lawyer, jurist, and author. He served both as Attorney General and Lord Chancellor of England. Although his political career ended in disgrace, he remained extremely influential through his works, especially as philosophical advocate and practitioner of the scientific revolution. His dedication brought him into a rare historical group of scientists who were killed by their own experiments. His works established and popularized an inductive methodology for scientific inquiry, often called the Baconian method or simply, the scientific method. His demand for a planned procedure of investigating all things natural marked a new turn in the rhetorical and theoretical framework for science, much of which still surrounds conceptions of proper methodology today. Bacon was knighted in 1603, created Baron Verulam in 1618, and Viscount St Alban in 1621; as he died without heirs both peerages became extinct upon his death.

In 1623 Bacon expressed his aspirations and ideals in *New Atlantis*. Released in 1627, this was his creation of an ideal land where "generosity and enlightenment, dignity and splendor, piety and public spirit" were the commonly held qualities of the inhabitants of Bensalem. In this work, he portrayed a vision of the future of human discovery and knowledge. The plan and organization of his ideal college, "Solomon's House", envisioned the modern research university in both applied and pure science.

The Baconian theory of Shakespearean authorship holds that Sir Francis Bacon wrote the plays conventionally attributed to William Shakespeare. The mainstream view is that William Shakespeare of Stratford, an actor in the Lord Chamberlain's Men (later the King's Men), wrote the poems and plays that bear his name. The Baconians, however, hold that scholars are so focused on the details of Shakespeare's life that they neglect to investigate the many facts that they see as connecting Bacon to the Shakespearean work. The main Baconian evidence is founded on the presentation of a motive for concealment, the circumstances surrounding the first known performance of *The Comedy of Errors*, the proximity of Bacon to the William Strachey letter upon which many scholars think *The Tempest* was based, perceived allusions in the plays to Bacon's legal acquaintances, the many supposed parallels with the plays of Bacon's published work and entries in the Promus (his private wastebook), Bacon's interest in civil histories, and ostensible autobiographical allusions in the plays. Because Bacon had first-hand knowledge of government cipher methods, most Baconians see it as feasible that he left his signature somewhere in the Shakespearean work. Supporters of the standard view, often referred to as "Stratfordian" or "Mainstream", dispute all contentions in favor of Bacon, and criticize Bacon's poetry as not being comparable in quality with that of Shakespeare.

Here's an essay by Francis Bacon, the first major English essayist, *Of Studies*:

Studies serve for delight, for ornament, and for ability. Their chief use for delight is in privateness and retiring; for ornament, is in discourse; and for ability, is in the judgment and disposition of business. For expert men can execute, and perhaps judge of particulars, one by one; but the general counsels, and the plots and marshalling of affairs, come best from those that are learned. To spend too much time in studies is sloth; to use them too much for ornament, is affectation; to make judgment wholly by their rules, is the humor of a scholar. They perfect nature, and are perfected by experience: for natural abilities are like natural plants, that need pruning, by study; and studies themselves do give forth directions too much at large, except they be bounded in by experience. Crafty men condemn studies, simple men admire them, and wise men use them; for they teach not their own use; but that is a wisdom without them, and above them, won by observation. Read not to contradict and confute; nor to believe and take for granted; nor to find talk and discourse; but to weigh and consider. Some books are to be tasted, others to be swallowed, and some few to be chewed and digested; that is, some books are to be read only in parts; others to be read, but not curiously; and some few to be read wholly, and with diligence and attention. Some books also may be read by deputy, and extracts made of them by others; but that would be only in the less important arguments, and the meaner sort of books, else distilled books are like common distilled waters, flashy things. Reading maketh a full man; conference a ready man; and writing an exact man. And therefore, if a man write little, he had need have a great memory; if he confer little, he had need have a present wit: and if he read little, he had need have much cunning, to seem to know that he doth not. Histories make men wise; poets witty; the mathematics subtle; natural philosophy deep; moral grave; logic and rhetoric able to contend. Abeunt studia in mores [Studies pass into and influence manners]. Nay, there is no stond or impediment in the wit but may be wrought out by fit studies; like as diseases of the body may have appropriate exercises. Bowling is good for the stone and reins; shooting for the lungs and breast; gentle walking for the stomach; riding for the head; and the like. So if a man's wit be wandering, let him study the mathematics; for in demonstrations, if his wit be called away never so little, he must begin again. If his wit be not apt to distinguish or find differences, let him study the Schoolmen; for they are cymini sectores [splitters of hairs]. If he be not apt to beat over matters, and to call up one thing to prove and illustrate another, let him study the lawyers' cases. So every defect of the mind may have a special receipt.

---

peerage: the rank of a British peer

ostensible: appearing or claiming to be one thing when it is really something else

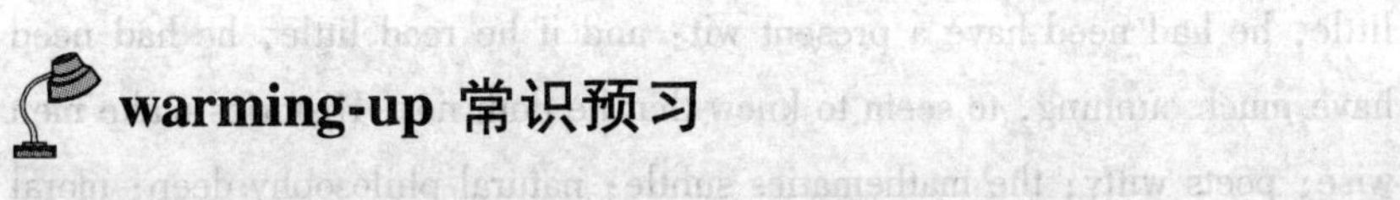

Unit Eight

warming-up 常识预习

1. "Nature made men happy and good, but society makes him evil and miserable." Who said this?

2. What play by Schiller is widely known in China?

3. Whose symphony Pastoral marked the beginning of the 19th century program music?

4. Who is the author of *Prometheus Unbound*?

5. The term "impressionism" first appeared in 1874 and from what was it taken directly?

6. Explain "a novel is a mirror walking along the road".

lecturette 专题讲座

Enlightenment, Romanticism and Realism

The Enlightenment is a term used to describe a time in Western philosophy and cultural life, centered upon the eighteenth century, in which reason was advocated as the primary source and legitimacy for authority. Developing more or less simultaneously in Germany, Great Britain, France, the Netherlands, Italy, Spain, and Portugal, and buoyed by the American colonists' successful rebellion against Great Britain in the American War of Independence, the culmination of the movement spread through much of Europe, including the Polish-Lithuanian Commonwealth, Russia and Scandinavia, along with Latin America and instigating the Haitian Revolution. It has been argued that the signatories of the American Declaration of Independence, the United States Bill of Rights, the French Declaration of the Rights of Man and of the Citizen, and the Polish-Lithuanian Constitution of May 3, 1791, were motivated by "Enlightenment" principles.

The term *Enlightenment* came into use in English during the mid-nineteenth century, with particular reference to French philosophy signifying generally the philosophical outlook of the eighteenth century. However, the German term *Aufklärung* was not merely applied retrospectively; it was already the common term by 1784, when Immanuel Kant published the influential essay "Answering the Question: What is Enlightenment?"

The Age of Enlightenment does not represent a single movement or school of thought, for these philosophies were often mutually contradictory or divergent. The Enlightenment was less a set of ideas than it was a set of values. At its core was a critical questioning of traditional institutions, customs, and morals. Thus, there was still a considerable degree of similarity between competing philosophies. Also, some philosophical schools of the period could not be considered part of the Enlightenment at all. Some classifications of this period also include the late seventeenth century, which is typically known as the Age of Reason or Age of Rationalism. There is no consensus on when to date the start of the age of Enlightenment and some scholars simply use the beginning of the eighteenth century or the middle of the seventeenth century as a default date. If taken back to the mid-1600s, the Enlightenment would trace its origins to Descartes' *Discourse on the Method* 1637. Others define the Enlightenment as beginning in Britain's Glorious Revolution of 1688 or with the publication of Isaac Newton's *Prin-*

cipia Mathematica which first appeared in 1687. As to its end, some scholars use the French Revolution of 1789 or the beginning of the Napoleonic Wars (1804—1815) as a convenient point in time with which to date the end of the Enlightenment.

The Enlightenment broke through the sacred circle, whose dogma had circumscribed thinking. The Enlightenment is held to be the source of critical ideas, such as the centrality of freedom, democracy, and reason as primary values of society. This view argues that the establishment of a contractual basis of rights would lead to the market mechanism and capitalism, the scientific method, religious tolerance, and the organization of states into self-governing republics through democratic means. In this view, the tendency of the philosophies in particular to apply rationality to every problem is considered the essential change. No brief summary can do justice to the diversity of enlightened thought in 18th-century Europe. Because it was a value system rather than a set of shared beliefs, there are many contradictory trains to follow. More broadly, the Enlightenment period is marked by increasing empiricism, scientific rigor, and reductionism, along with increasing questioning of religious orthodoxy. A variety of 19th-century movements, including liberalism and neo-classicism, traced their intellectual heritage back to the Enlightenment.

Romanticism is a complex artistic, literary, and intellectual movement that originated in the second half of the 18th century in Western Europe, and gained strength in reaction to the Industrial Revolution. In part, it was a revolt against aristocratic social and political norms of the Age of Enlightenment and a reaction against the scientific rationalization of nature, and was embodied most strongly in the visual arts, music, and literature, but can be detected even in changed attitudes towards children and education. The movement validated strong emotion as an authentic source of aesthetic experience, placing new emphasis on such emotions as trepidation, horror and terror and awe—especially that which is experienced in confronting the sublimity of untamed nature and its picturesque qualities, both new aesthetic categories. It elevated folk art and ancient custom to something noble, made of spontaneity a desirable character (as in the musical impromptu), and argued for a "natural" epistemology of human activities as conditioned by nature in the form of language and customary usage. Romanticism reached beyond the rational and Classicist ideal models to elevate a revived medievalism and elements of art and narrative perceived to be authentically medieval, in an attempt to escape the confines of population growth, urban sprawl, and industrialism, and it also attempted to embrace the exotic, unfamiliar, and distant in modes more authentic than Rococo chinoiserie, harnessing the power of the imagination to envision and to escape. The modern sense of a romantic character may be expressed in Byronic ideals of a gifted, perhaps misunderstood loner, creatively following the dictates of his inspiration rather than the mores of contemporary society.

Although the movement is rooted in the German Sturm und Drang movement, which prized intuition and emotion over Enlightenment rationalism, the ideologies and events of the French Revolution laid the background from which both Romanticism and the Counter-Enlightenment emerged. The confines of the Industrial Revolution also had their influence on Romanticism, which was in part an escape from modern realities; indeed, in the second half of the 19th century, "Realism" was offered as a polarized opposite to Romanticism. Romanticism elevated the achievements of what it perceived as heroic individualists and artists, whose pioneering examples would elevate society. It also legitimized the individual imagination as a critical authority, which permitted freedom from classical notions of form in art. There was a strong recourse to historical and natural inevitability, a zeitgeist, in the representation of its ideas.

Realism is a literary term which is so widely used as to be more or less meaningless except when used in contradistinction to some other movement, such as Naturalism, Expressionism, Surrealism. The original definition of realism by Sir P. Harvey was "a loosely used term meaning truth to the observed facts of life (especially when they are gloomy)." Realism has been chiefly concerned with the commonplaces of everyday life among the middle and lower classes, where character is a product of social factors and environment is the integral element in the dramatic complications. Realism in literature is an approach that attempts to describe life without idealization or romantic subjectivity. Although realism is not limited to any one century or group of writers, it is most often associated with the literary movement in 19th-century France, specifically with the French novelists Flaubert and Balzac. In the drama, realism is most closely associated with Ibsen's social plays. Later writers felt that realism laid too much emphasis on external reality. Many, notably Henry James, turned to a psychological realism that closely examined the complex workings of the mind (stream of consciousness). The French realist school of the mid-19th century stressed "sincerity" as opposed to the "liberty" proclaimed by the Romantics; it insisted on accurate documentation, sociological insight, an accumulation of the details of material fact, an avoidance of poetic diction, idealization, exaggeration, melodrama, etc.; subjects were to be taken from everyday life, preferably from lower-class life. This emphasis clearly reflected the interests of an increasingly positivist and scientific age. French Realism developed into Naturalism, an associated but more scientifically applied and elaborated doctrine, seen by some later critics (notably Marxist critics) as degenerate. George Eliot introduced realism into England (William Dean Howells introduced it into the United States). In England, the French realists were imitated consciously and notably by George Augustus Moore and Arnold Bennett, but the English novel from the time of Defoe had had its own unlabelled strain of realism, and the term is thus applied to English literature in varying senses and contexts, sometimes qualified as "social" or "psychological" realism etc.

Realism in literature and the visual arts is the depiction of subjects as they appear in everyday life, without embellishment or interpretation. The term also describes works of art which, in revealing a truth, may emphasize the ugly or sordid. Realism often refers to the artistic movement, which began in France in the 1850s. The popularity of realism grew with the introduction of photography—a new visual source that created a desire for people to produce things that look "objectively real." Realists positioned themselves against romanticism, a genre dominating French literature and artwork in the late 18th and early nineteenth century. Undistorted by personal bias, Realism believed in the ideology of objective reality and revolted against exaggerated emotionalism. Truth and accuracy became the goals of many Realists. Many paintings which sprung up during the time of realism depicted people at their jobs, because during the 19th century there were many open work places due to the Industrial Revolution and Commercial Revolutions. Realists render everyday characters, situations, dilemmas, and objects, all in a "true-to-life" manner. Realists tend to discard theatrical drama, lofty subjects and classical forms of art in favor of commonplace themes. The achievement of realism in theatre was to direct attention to the physical and philosophic problems of ordinary existence, both socially and psychologically. In plays of this mode people emerge as victims of forces larger than themselves, as individuals confronted with a rapidly accelerating world. These pioneering playwrights were unafraid to present their characters as ordinary, impotent, and unable to arrive at answers to their predicaments. This type of art represents what we see with our human eyes.

---

culmination：巅峰

instigate：cause to happen

signatory：one of the people, organizations, or countries that signs an official agreement

circumscribe：restrict

sublimity：nobility in thought or feeling or style

impromptu：done or said without any preparation or planning

Rococo：a style of 18th century French art and interior design 洛可可艺术

chinoiserie：a style in art reflecting Chinese artistic influence

mores：the customs, social behavior, and moral values of a particular group

zeitgeist：the general spirit or feeling of a period in history

in contradistinction to：in contrast to or compared to

positivist：实证哲学家,实证主义者

sordid：involving immoral or dishonest behaviour

reductionism：还原论(主张把高级运动形式还原为低级运动形式的一种哲学观点)

epistemology：a branch of philosophy concerning the nature and scope of knowledge 认识论

Sturm und Drang：(十八世纪德国文学上的)狂飙运动

Descartes：笛卡尔(1596—1690,著名的法国哲学家、数学家、物理学家)

George Eliot：pen name of the English novelist Mary Evans (1819—1880)

going-over 复习反馈

multiple-choice Q's

1. The term "Enlightenment" came into use in English during ______ century.

A. the late eighteenth B. the mid-nineteenth

C. the early twentieth

2. Rococo is a style of ______ century French art.

A. the eighteenth B. the nineteenth C. the twentieth

3. The popularity of ______ grew with the introduction of photography.

A. realism B. romanticism C. enlightenment

4. Some realist school stressed "______" as opposed to the "liberty" proclaimed by the Romantics.

A. captivity B. suppression C. sincerity

5. What cultural movement in Western Europe gained strength in reaction to the Industrial Revolution?

A. Realism. B. Romanticism. C. Enlightenment.

6. French ______ developed into Naturalism.

A. Realism B. Romanticism C. Enlightenment

7. Who introduced realism into England?

A. Arnold Bennett B. William Dean Howells.

C. George Eliot.

8. The Age of Reason can be classified into ______.

A. Realism B. Romanticism C. Enlightenment

9. Enlightenment developed almost simultaneously in Germany, Great Britain, France, the Netherlands, ______.

A. Italy, Spain, and Greece
B. Italy, Spain, and Portugal
C. Italy, Spain, and Turkey

essay Q's

10. Talk about your understanding of the cultural movement Enlightenment in Europe.

11. Talk about your understanding of the cultural movement Romanticism in Europe.

12. Talk about your understanding of the cultural movement Realism in Europe.

assignments 课题作业

Prepare a brief summary on the classical music. This assignment may be presented either as a written text or orally in class next time.

extensions 自主拓展

Learn after-class the Romanticism in literature. This text is included mainly as entertainment. What novel have you read from American romantic Gothic literature Romanticism?

In literature, Romanticism found recurrent themes in the evocation or criticism of the past, the cult of "sensibility" with its emphasis on women and children, the heroic isolation of the artist or narrator, and respect for a new, wilder, untrammeled and "pure" nature. Furthermore, several romantic authors, such as Edgar Allan Poe and Nathaniel Hawthorne, based their writings on the supernatural / occult and human psychology. Romanticism also helped in the emergence of new ideas and in the process led to the emergence of positive voices that were beneficial for the marginalized sections of the society.

The Scottish poet James Macpherson influenced the early development of Romanticism with the international success of his Ossian cycle of poems published in 1762, inspiring both Goethe and the young Walter Scott. Romanticism in British literature developed in a different form slightly later, mostly associated with the poets William Wordsworth and Samuel Taylor Coleridge, whose co-authored book *Lyrical Ballads* (1798) sought to reject Augustan poetry in favor of more direct speech derived from folk traditions. Both poets were also involved in utopian social thought in the wake of the French Revolution. The poet and painter William Blake is the most extreme example of the Romantic sensibility in Britain, epitomized by his claim "I must create a system or be enslaved by another man's." Blake's artistic work is also strongly influenced by Medieval illuminated books. The painters J. M. W. Turner and John Constable are also generally associated with Romanticism. Lord Byron, Percy Bysshe Shelley, Mary Shelley and John Keats constitute another phase of Romanticism in Britain.

In predominantly Roman Catholic countries Romanticism was less pronounced than in Germany and Britain, and tended to develop later, after the rise of Napoleon. François-René de Chateaubriand is often called the "Father of French Romanticism". In France, the movement is associated with the nineteenth century, particularly in the paintings of Théodore Géricault and Eugène Delacroix, the plays, poems and novels of Victor Hugo (such as *Les Misérables* and *Ninety-Three*), and the novels of Stendhal.

In the United States, romantic Gothic literature made an early appearance with Washington Irving's *The Legend of Sleepy Hollow* and *Rip Van Winkle* (1819), followed by *The Leatherstocking Tales* of James Fenimore Cooper, with their emphasis on heroic simplicity and their fervent landscape descriptions of an already-exotic mythicized frontier peopled by "noble savages", similar to the philosophical theory of Rousseau, exemplified by Uncas, from *The Last of the Mohicans*. There are picturesque "local color" elements in Washington Irving's essays and especially his travel books. Edgar Allan Poe's tales of the macabre and his balladic poetry were more influential in France than at home, but the romantic American novel developed fully in Nathaniel Hawthorne's atmosphere and melodrama. Later Transcendentalist writers such as Henry David Thoreau and Ralph Waldo Emerson still show elements of its influence and imagination, as does the romantic realism of Walt Whitman. But by the 1880s, psychological and social realism was competing with romanticism in the novel. The poetry of Emily Dickinson—nearly unread in her own time—and Herman Melville's novel *Moby-Dick* can be taken as epitomes of American Romantic literature.

Romantics frequently shared certain general characteristics: moral enthusiasm, faith in the value of individualism and intuitive perception, and a presumption that the natural world is a source of goodness and human society a source of corruption.

Romanticism became popular in American politics, philosophy and art. The movement appealed to the revolutionary spirit of America as well as to those longing to break free of the strict religious traditions of early settlement. The Romantics rejected rationalism and religious intellect. It appealed to those in opposition of Calvinism, which involved the belief that the universe and all the events within it are subject to the power of God. The Romantic Movement gave rise to New England Transcendentalism which portrayed a less restrictive relationship between God and Universe. The new religion presented the individual with a more personal relationship with God. Transcendentalism and Romanticism appealed to Americans in a similar fashion.

As a moral philosophy, transcendentalism was neither logical nor systemized. It exalted feeling over reason, individual expression over the restraints of law and custom. It appealed to those who disdained the harsh God of their Puritan ancestors, and it appealed to those who scorned the pale deity of New England Unitarianism. They spoke for cultural rejuvenation and against the materialism of American society. They believed in the transcendence of the "Oversoul", an all-pervading power for goodness from which all things come and of which all things are parts. American Romance embraced the individual and rebelled against the confinement of neoclassicism and religious tradition. The Romantic Movement in America created a new literary genre that continues to influence modern writers. Novels, short stories, and poems began to take the place of the sermons and manifestos that were associated with the early American literary principles. Romantic literature was personal, intense, and portrayed more emotion than ever seen in neoclassical literature. America's preoccupation with freedom became a great source of motivation for Romantic writers as many were delighted in free expression and emotion without so much fear of ridicule and controversy. They also put more effort into the psychological development of their characters. "Heroes and heroines exhibited extremes of sensitivity and excitement"

---

recurrent: happening or appearing several times

untrammeled: not limited by anyone or anything

occult: magical and mysterious

epitomize: be a typical example of

macabre: shockingly repellent; inspiring horror

transcendentalism: the belief that knowledge can be obtained by studying thought rather than by practical experience 超验主义

unitarianism: a Nontrinitarian Christian theology which teaches belief, in the single personality of God, in contrast to the doctrine of the Trinity (God as three persons). 唯一神教派(教义)

manifesto: a written statement by a political party, saying what they believe in and what they intend to do

Edgar Allan Poe: American writer (1809—1849)

Johann Wolfgang von Goethe: a German writer and polymath (1749—1832)

Victor-Marie Hugo: a French poet, playwright, novelist, essayist, visual artist, statesman, human rights activist and exponent of the Romantic movement in France (1802—1885)

Jean-Jacques Rousseau: a major Genevois philosopher, writer, and composer of the 18th-century Enlightenment (1712—1778)

Unit Nine

warming-up 常识预习

1. What do the characters which make up Japan's name mean?

2. What date is the Victory over Japan Day?

3. What do you know about Japan's indigenous concepts of business culture such as nemawashi, nenko system, salaryman, and office lady?

4. Is karaoke the most widely practiced cultural activity in Japan?

5. Do people of all ages in Japan read manga?

6. Why are there often strong earthquakes to shake the islands of Japan?

lecturette 专题讲座

The Indigenous Development of Japan

Western World, when referring to current events, the term often includes developed countries in Asia, such as Japan, Singapore, and South Korea, which have strong economic, political and military ties to Western Europe, NATO or the United States. While these countries also have substantial Western influence and similarities in their cultures, they nonetheless maintain largely different and distinctive cultures, religions (though Christianity is a major religion in South Korea), languages, customs, and worldviews that are products of their own indigenous development, rather than solely Western influences.

Japan is an island country in East Asia. Located in the Pacific Ocean, it lies to the east of the Sea of Japan, the People's Republic of China, North Korea, South Korea and Russia, stretching from the Sea of Okhotsk in the north to the East China Sea. Japan has the world's tenth-largest population, with about 128 million people. The Greater Tokyo Area, which includes the de facto capital city of Tokyo and several surrounding prefectures, is the largest metropolitan area in the world, with over 30 million residents.

The English word Japan is an exonym. The Japanese names for Japan are Nippon and Nihon. The Japanese name Nippon is used for most official purposes, including on Japanese money, postage stamps, and for many international sporting events. Nihon is a more casual term and the most frequently used in contemporary speech. Japanese people refer to themselves as Nihonjin and they call their language Nihongo. Both Nippon and Nihon literally mean "the sun's origin" and are often translated as "the Land of the Rising Sun". This nomenclature comes from Imperial correspondence with the Chinese Sui Dynasty and refers to Japan's eastward position relative to China. Before Japan had relations with China, it was known as Yamato and Hi no moto, which means "source of the sun". The English word for Japan came to the West from early trade routes. The early Mandarin or possibly Wu Chinese word for Japan was recorded by Marco Polo as Cipangu. In modern Shanghainese, a Wu dialect, the pronunciation of characters is Zeppen.

Japan's feudal era was characterized by the emergence of a ruling class of warriors, the samurai. During the sixteenth century, traders and Jesuit missionaries from Portugal reached Japan for the first time, initiating active commercial and cultural exchange between Japan and the West.

The study of Western sciences, known as rangaku, continued through contacts with the Dutch. On March 31, 1854, Commodore Matthew Perry and the "Black Ships" of the United States Navy forced the opening of Japan to the outside world with the Convention of Kanagawa. Subsequent similar treaties with the Western countries in the Bakumatsu period brought Japan into economic and political crises. The abundance of the prerogative and the resignation of the shogunate led to the Boshin War and the establishment of a centralized state unified under the name of the Emperor. Adopting Western political, judicial and military institutions, the Cabinet organized the Privy Council, introduced the Meiji Constitution, and assembled the Imperial Diet. The Meiji Restoration transformed the Empire of Japan into an industrialized world power that embarked on a number of military conflicts to expand the nation's sphere of influence. After victories in the First Sino-Japanese War (1894—1895) and the Russo-Japanese War (1904—1905), Japan gained control of Chinese Taiwan, Korea, and the southern half of Sakhalin.

The early twentieth century saw a brief period of "Taisho democracy" overshadowed by the rise of expansionism and militarization. World War I enabled Japan, which joined the side of the victorious Allies, to expand its influence and territorial holdings. Japan continued its expansionist policy by occupying Manchuria in 1931. As a result of international condemnation for this occupation, Japan resigned from the League of Nations two years later. In 1936, Japan signed the Anti-Comintern Pact with Nazi Germany, joining the Axis powers in 1941. In 1941, Japan signed the Soviet-Japanese Neutrality Pact with Soviet Union, respecting both Manchukou and Mongolian People's Republic territories. In 1937, Japan invaded other parts of China, precipitating the Second Sino-Japanese War (1937—

1945), after which the United States placed an oil embargo on Japan. On December 7, 1941, Japan attacked the United States naval base in Pearl Harbor and declared war on the United States and the United Kingdom. On December 8, Netherlands declared war on Japan. This act brought the United States into World War II. After the atomic bombings of Hiroshima and Nagasaki in 1945, along with the Soviet Union joining the war against it, Japan agreed to an unconditional surrender of all Japanese forces on August 15. In 1947, Japan adopted a new pacifist constitution emphasizing liberal democratic practices. The Allied occupation ended by the Treaty of San Francisco in 1952 and Japan was granted membership in the United Nations in 1956. Japan later achieved spectacular growth to become the second largest economy in the world, with an annual growth rate averaging 10% for four decades. This ended in the mid-1990s when Japan suffered a major recession. Positive growth in the early twenty-first century has signaled a gradual recovery.

Japan is a constitutional monarchy where the power of the Emperor is very limited. As a ceremonial figurehead, he is defined by the constitution as "the symbol of the state and of the unity of the people". Power is held chiefly by the Prime Minister of Japan and other elected members of the Diet, while sovereignty is vested in the Japanese people. The Emperor effectively acts as the head of state on diplomatic occasions. Akihito is the current Emperor of Japan. Naruhito, Crown Prince of Japan, stands as next in line to the throne. The Prime Minister of Japan is the head of government. The position is appointed by the Emperor of Japan after being designated by the Diet from among its members and must enjoy the confidence of the House of Representatives to remain in office. The Prime Minister is the head of the Cabinet (the literal translation of his Japanese title is "Prime Minister of the Cabinet") and appoints and dismisses the Ministers of

State, a majority of whom must be Diet members.

Japan's military is restricted by the Article 9 of the Japanese Constitution, which renounces Japan's right to declare war or use military force as a means of settling international disputes. Japan's military is governed by the Ministry of Defense, and primarily consists of the Japan Ground Self-Defense Force (JGSDF), the Japan Maritime Self-Defense Force (JMSDF) and the Japan Air Self-Defense Force (JASDF).

Japan consists of forty-seven prefectures, each overseen by an elected governor, legislature and administrative bureaucracy. Each prefecture is further divided into cities, towns and villages. Mount Fuji, cherry blossom trees and a shinkansen in the foreground—all three are iconic of Japan.

Japan is a country of over three thousand islands extending along the Pacific coast of Asia. The main islands, running from north to south, are Hokkaido, Honshu (the main island), Shikoku and Kyushu. The Ryukyu Islands, including Okinawa, are a chain of islands south of Kyushu. Together they are often known as the Japanese Archipelago. Its location on the Pacific Ring of Fire, at the juncture of three tectonic plates, gives Japan frequent low-intensity tremors and occasional volcanic activity. Destructive earthquakes, often resulting in tsunamis, occur several times each century. It sometimes experiences extremely hot temperatures because of the foehn wind phenomenon.

Primary, secondary schools and universities were introduced into Japan in 1872 as a result of the Meiji Restoration. Since 1947, compulsory education in Japan consists of elementary school and middle school, which lasts for nine years (from age 6 to age 15). Almost all children continue their education at a three-year senior high school, and, according to the MEXT, about 75.9% of high school graduates attend a university, junior college, trade school, or other post-secondary institution in 2005. Japan's education is very competitive, especially for entrance to institutions of higher education. The two top-ranking universities in Japan are the University of Tokyo and Kyoto University. The Programme for International Student Assessment, coordinated by the OECD, currently ranks Japanese knowledge and skills of 15-year-old as the 6th best in the world.

In Japan, English-language education (eigo-kyouiku) starts the first year of junior high school and continues at least until the third year of high school. Surprisingly students are still unable to speak or to comprehend English properly after this time. One of the reasons is the instruction focusing on the skill of reading and writing. In the past, Japan was a nation composed of a single ethnic group and had very small number of foreign visitors, and there were few opportunities to converse in a foreign language, therefore the study of foreign languages was mainly considered to obtain the knowledge from the literature of other countries. Learning English became popular after World War II, but English was taught by teachers who were trained under the method that emphasized reading. There were no qualified teachers to teach listening and speaking. Another reason lies in the Ministry of Education's guidelines. The guideline limits the English vocabulary that is to be learned during the three years junior high school to about 1,000 words. Textbooks must be screened first by the Ministry of Education, resulting for the most part in standardized textbooks, which makes English language learning too confining. However, in recent years the necessity of communicating in English has increased as the ability to listen to and speak English is in demand. The students and adults who study English conversation have increased rapidly in number and private English conversation schools have become prominent. Schools are now also putting strength into eigo-kyouiku by the installation of language laboratories and the hiring of foreign language teachers.

prefecture：district

exonym：外来名称

nomenclature：命名法

prerogative：privilege

shogunate：将军职位，将军政治，幕府时代

Manchuria：满洲（我国东北的旧称）

Hiroshima：广岛

Nagasaki：长崎

The Diet (of Japan)：日本国国会

shinkansen：（日本）高速客运列车，新干线

Hokkaido：北海道（日本第二大岛）

Honshu：本州（日本最大的岛屿）

Shikoku：四国（日本主要岛屿之一）

Kyushu：九州（日本）

archipelago：群岛

tectonic plate：（地球表面的构造板块）

tsunami：a wave train, a series of water waves

foehn：a type of dry down-slope wind which occurs in the lee of a mountain range 焚风

going-over 复习反馈

multiple-choice Q's

1. The cultural exchange between Japan and the West started from the ______ century.

A. fifteenth　　B. sixteenth　　C. seventeenth

2. ______ of Japan is the head of government.

A. The Emperor B. The Prime Minister

C. The Crown Prince

3. Japan's feudal era was characterized by a ______ ruling class.

A. Nihonjin B. warrior C. ninja

4. Christianity is a major religion in ______.

A. Japan B. Singapore C. South Korea

5. During World War II, the United States conducted two atomic bombings against Japan in the cities of ______.

A. Hiroshima and Nagasaki B. Hokkaido and Okinawa

C. Shikoku and Kyushu

6. The Japanese study of Western sciences went through contacts with ______.

A. the Dutch B. the Portuguese

C. the Americans

7. Japan has the world's ______ -largest population.

A. eighth B. ninth C. tenth

8. Nippon is used for Japanese ______.

A. money B. language C. correspondence

9. Which of the following is iconic of Japan?

A. Okhotsk. B. Eigo-kyouiku. C. Shinkansen.

essay Q's

10. For what does Western World often include Japan?

11. What movement made Japan an industrialized world power?

12. Talk about the English-language education in Japan.

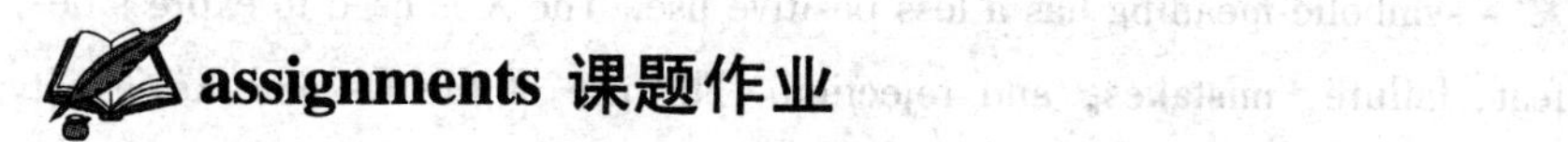

assignments 课题作业

Prepare a brief summary on the rise of Japan in the Western World. This assignment may be presented either as a written text or orally in class next time.

extensions 自主拓展

Learn after-class something of the Japanese way. This text is included mainly as entertainment. Can you find anything similar in China?

The Japanese have traditionally sat on tatami (a padded straw mat) at their homes. However, many homes today are completely Western style and don't have Japanese style rooms with tatami. Many young Japanese are no longer able to sit properly on tatami. The proper way of sitting on tatami is called seiza. It is to bend the knees 180 degrees tuck your calves under your thighs and sit on your heels. This can be a difficult posture to maintain if you are not used to it and requires practice, preferably from early age. It is considered polite to sit seiza style on formal occasions. Another more relaxed way of sitting is cross-legged (agura). Starting with legs out straight and folding them in like triangles. This posture is usually for men. Women would usually go from the formal to an informal sitting posture by shifting their feet just off to the side (yokozuwari). Though most Japanese do not concern themselves with it, it is proper to walk without stepping in the edge of the tatami.

Os and Xs have a special meaning in Japan. The circle's symbolic meaning covers such things as: correct, passing, winning, and OK. The X's symbolic meaning has a less positive use. The X is used to express defeat, failure, mistakes, and rejection. The use of the Os and Xs is not merely limited to physical gestures, and one can also find them in writing. An example of this would be a true false test where O = true and X = false. When one forms the circle, one uses both the thumb and forefinger, or one can raise one's arms above one's head so that one's fingers are touching. The X is formed by crossing forefingers, or by making an X with one's arms. Sometimes when someone makes the X signal it is followed by the word "dame," which means bad, or no good.

When Japanese count on their fingers they use only one hand. Counting from one through five starts with the thumb, then proceeds to the pinky. Each finger is folded down as it is counted. Six through ten are counted on the same hand in the reverse order, opening the fingers as they are counted. This is the most common method used in Japan regardless of age or sex. When indicating numbers to another, a Japanese person will raise his/her palm, facing the other person, and raise the appropriate fingers starting with the forefinger, middle finger, ring finger, and pinky. The thumb is used last, and the second hand will be added for numbers over five.

April 29th is Japan's National holiday, Showa no hi. This day leads Japan into Golden Week, a succession of holidays. When Saturdays and

Sundays are included, this week becomes one of the longest holidays of the year. The weather is warm and suitable for excursions at this time, therefore many Japanese make trips during Golden Week and it is one of the busiest travel times. Showa no hi (Showa Day) April 29: It used to be Emperor Showa's birthday celebration. After his death in 1989, it was designated as "Midori no hi (Greenery Day)," a day for the appreciation of nature. It was decided to change the name of this day to "Showa no hi". Kenpo kinenbi (Constitution Day) May 3: The present Constitution of Japan was put into effect on this day in 1947. Midori no hi (Greenery Day) May 4: "Midori no hi" used to be celebrated on April 29, until 2006. Before being declared "Midori no hi," May 4 was a national holiday as it falls between two other holidays. Kodomo no hi (Children's Day) May 5: A day to wish for the health and happiness of children. Some companies give employees a day off on May 1, which is May Day.

The cherry blossom (sakura) is the national flower of Japan. It is probably most beloved flower among the Japanese. The blooming of cherry blossoms signifies not only the arrival of spring but the beginning of the new academic year for schools (April) and of the new fiscal year for businesses. Sakura is symbol of a bright future. Also, their delicacy suggests purity, transience, melancholy and has poetic appeal. During this period, the weather forecasts include reports on the advance of sakura zensen (sakura front) as the blossoms sweep north. As the trees begin to bloom, the Japanese participate in hanami (flower viewing). People gather under the trees, eat picnic lunches, drink sake, view the flowers and have a great time. In cities, viewing sakura in the evening (yozakura) is also popular. Against the dark sky, sakura in full bloom are especially beautiful. However, there is also a dark side. Sakura open all at once and seldom last more than a week. From the way they quickly and gracefully fall, they were used by militarism to beautify the death of the suicide units. To samurai in the ancient times or soldiers during World Wars there was no greater glory than dying on the battlefield like scattered sakura. Sakura-yu is a tea-like drink made by steeping a salt-preserved cherry blossom in hot water. It is often served at wedding and other auspicious occasions. Sakura-mochi is a dumpling containing sweet bean paste wrapped in a salt-preserved cherry-tree leaf. A sakura also means a shill who raves about his mock purchase. Originally referring to people who were admitted to watch plays for free, the word came about because cherry blossoms are free for viewing. Sakura is synonymous with the word "flower (hana)". Hana yori dango (dumplings over flowers) is a proverb that expresses the practical is preferred over the aesthetic. In hanami, people often seem to be more interested in eating foods or drinking alcohol than appreciating the beauty of the flowers.

Also, some behaviors are seen as being rude by Japanese standards.

1) It is considered a shameful act to kiss in public.

2) Hugging is considered impolite in Japan.

3) It is considered rude to be the only person eating something.

4) One should always take off their shoes when entering a Japanese house or restaurant (you will most often be supplied with slippers).

---

pinky = pinkie: little finger
Showa no hi: 昭和日
sakura: 樱花
samurai: 日本武士

Unit Ten

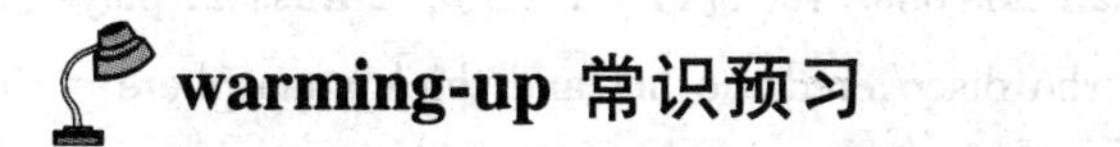

warming-up 常识预习

1. How good does your language have to be to study in a European university?

2. Which European institution of higher learning is the oldest?

3. What's your dream university in Europe for further studies?

4. What are the barriers around universities in Europe?

5. What's the problem with Europe's universities?

6. Which are the best universities for studying medicine in Europe?

lecturette 专题讲座

University Rankings in Europe

University of Cambridge (founded 1209) and University of Oxford (founded 1096) of the United Kingdom are ranked among the best in the world, according to a higher education web directory and search engine of world-wide Universities and Colleges.

Commonly, the 3rd one on the list of 2010 Top 100 Universities and Colleges in Europe is ETH Zurich, (Eidgenössische Technische Hochschule Zürich in German, or Swiss Federal Institute of Technology Zurich in English) founded in 1855. It is a science and technology university in the

City of Zurich, Switzerland. Locals sometimes refer to it by the name Poly, derived from the original name Eidgenössisches Polytechnikum or Federal Polytechnic Institute. The 4th one on the list is Lomonosov Moscow State University. Founded in 1755, it is the oldest university in Russia and has the tallest educational building in the world. The university was named in honor of its founder, Mikhail Lomonosov (1711—1765), a Russian polymath, scientist and poet, who discovered the hot and thick atmosphere of Venus and created the basis of the modern Russian literary language. The 5th and 6th are of Spain, Complutense University of Madrid (UCM, founded 1499) and University of Granada (UGR, founded 1531). The 7th on the list is Tampere University of Technology (TUT, or TTY in Finnish, founded 1965), which is Finland's largest university in engineering sciences located in Hervanta, a suburb of Tampere. It has close ties to many different companies like Nokia. Imperial College of London (founded 1907) goes the 8th on the list. Next is the University of Zurich (UZH, founded 1833), which is the largest university in Switzerland. No. 10 is the Eotvos Lorand University (ELTE), the oldest and largest university in Hungary, located in Budapest. The university was founded in 1635 by an archbishop. Leadership was given over to the Jesuits. At this time, the university only had two colleges (College of Arts and College of Theology). The College of Law was added in 1667 and the College of Medicine was started in 1769. After the dissolution of the Jesuit order, the university was moved to Buda (a part of Budapest today) in 1777 in accordance with the intention of the founder. The university received its final location in Pest (the other side of today's Budapest) in 1784. The language of education was Latin until 1844, when Hungarian was introduced as an official language. Women have been allowed to enroll since 1895. It was named University of Budapest. The Science Division started its separate life in 1949.

The university received its current name in 1950 after the Hungarian physicist Baron Lorand Eotvos (1848—1919, more commonly called Baron Roland von Eotvos in the English literature) who is remembered today largely for his work on gravitation and surface tension.

Royal Institute of Technology (KTH, founded 1827) is the 13th on the list, and University of Oslo (UiO, founded 1811) the 30th (World University Ranking 133rd). They are Scandinavian.

Germans have the 15th and 16th on the list of 2010 Top 100, Free University of Berlin (FUB, founded 1948) and University of Leipzig (1409). While the French have the 59th (197th World), Caen University (founded 1432).

University of Bergen (UiB, founded 1946) is the 100th on the list of 2010 Top 100 Universities and Colleges in Europe, which is 275th in the world.

Well, no. One on the list of Top 200 World University Ranking, is Massachusetts Institute of Technology, founded in 1861. Stanford University is the 2nd on the list, founded in 1885; and Harvard University the 3rd, founded in 1636. No. 5 is University of California, Berkeley (1868); University of Pennsylvania (1740) the 7th; Cornell University (1865) the 8th; Yale University (1701) the 10th. They are of the United States. Cornell University is a private university located in Ithaca, New York, that is also a member of the Ivy League.

The 4th one on the list is the National Autonomous University of Mexico (UNAM, founded 1551). This is a public university based primarily in Mexico City and generally considered to be the largest one-campus university in the Americas in terms of student population. Originally the Roman Catholic-sponsored Royal and Pontifical University of Mexico was founded by a royal decree of Charles I of Spain. UNAM is the only university in Mexico with Nobel Prize laureates among its alumni: Alfonso García Robles (Peace), Octavio Paz (Literature), and Mario Molina (Chemistry). Besides being one of the most recognized universities in Latin America, it is one of the largest and the most artistically detailed. Its main campus is a World Heritage site that was designed by some of Mexico's best-known architects of the 20th century. Murals in the main campus were painted by some of the most recognized artists in Mexican history, such as Diego Rivera and David Alfaro Siqueiros.

The 6th on the list of Top 200 World University Ranking is Peking University, founded in 1898. The 9th is Shanghai Jiao Tong University (1896) (SJTU). Tsinghua University (1911) is No. 11.

The University of Bologna (UNIBO) is the oldest continually operating degree-granting university in Europe. The word *universitas* was first used by this institution at its foundation. The true date of its founding is uncertain, but believed by most accounts to have been 1088. Since 2000, the University's motto has been *Alma mater studiorum* (Latin for "fostering mother of studies"). The university received a charter from Frederick I Barbarossa in 1158, but in the 19th century, a committee of historians led by Giosue Carducci traced the founding of the University back to 1088, making it arguably the oldest university in the world. The university is historically notable for its teaching of canon and civil law. Until modern times, the only degree granted at that university was the doctorate. The University counts about 100,000 students in its 23 faculties. It has branch centers in Reggio Emilia, Imola, Ravenna, Forli, Cesena and Rimini and a branch center abroad in Buenos Aires. Moreover, it has a school of excellence named Collegio Superiore di Bologna.

Higher education processes are being harmonized across the European Community. Nowadays the University offers 128 different "Laurea" or

"Laurea breve" first-level degrees (three years of courses), followed by a similar number of "Laurea specialistica" specialized degrees (two years). However, some courses have maintained preceding rules of "Laurea specialistica europea" or "Laurea magistrale", with only one cycle of study of five years, except for medicine which requires six years of courses. After the "Laurea" one may attain 1st level Master. After "Laurea specialistica" and "Laurea specialistica europea" are attained, one may proceed to 2nd level Master, specialization schools, or doctorates of research.

In early 1950s some students of the University of Bologna were among the founders of the review "il Mulino". On April 25, 1951, was published in Bologna the first issue of the review. In a short time, "il Mulino" became one of the most interesting reference points in Italy for the political and cultural debate, and established important editorial relationships in Italy and abroad. Editorial activities evolved along with the review: in 1954 was founded the il Mulino publishing house (Societa editrice il Mulino) that today represents one of the most relevant Italian publishers. Besides, were initiated research projects (focusing mostly on the educational institutions and the political system in Italy), that eventually led, in 1964, to the establishment of the Istituto Carlo Cattaneo.

The University of Oslo (Norwegian: Universitetet i Oslo, Latin: Universitas Osloensis) is the oldest, largest and most prestigious university in Norway, situated in the Norwegian capital of Oslo. It was founded in 1811 as The Royal Frederick University (in Norwegian Det Kongelige Frederiks Universitet and in Latin Universitas Regia Fredericiana). The university was modeled after the recently established University of Berlin, and originally named after King Frederick of Denmark and Norway. It received its current name in 1939.

The university has faculties of (Lutheran) Theology, Law, Medicine,

Humanities, Mathematics and Natural Sciences, Dentistry, Social Sciences, and Education. The Faculty of Law is still located at the old campus on Karl Johans gate, near the National Theatre, the Royal Palace and the Parliament, while most of the other faculties are located at a modern campus area called Blindern, erected from the 1930s. The Faculty of Medicine is split between several university hospitals in the Oslo area. Currently the university has about 27,000 students and employs about 4,600 people. It is considered one of the leading universities of Scandinavia, and is consistently ranked among the world's top 100 or top 200 universities. In 2007 the University of Oslo was ranked as the best university in Norway, the 19th best in Europe and 69th best in the world in the Academic Ranking of World Universities. Also, in 2005 its faculty of humanities was ranked as the best in the Nordic countries, the 5th best in Europe and the 16th best in the world by the Times Higher Education Supplement. In 2009, the university was ranked as the 101st best in the world by Times Higher Education. Until the founding of the University in 1811, the University of Copenhagen was the only university of Denmark-Norway. After the dissolution of the Dano-Norwegian union in 1814, close academic ties between the countries have been maintained. The University of Oslo was the only university in Norway until 1946, and hence informally often known as simply "The University". The University of Oslo is home to five Nobel Prize winners, with one of the Nobel Prizes (the Nobel Peace Prize) itself being awarded in the city of Oslo, close to the Faculty of Law.

The seal of the University of Oslo features Apollo with the Lyre, and dates from 1835. The seal has been redesigned several times, most recently in 2009. The former design dates from the 1980s.

Like all public institutions of higher education in Norway, the university does not charge tuition fees. However, a small fee of NOK 420 (roughly US $65) per term goes to the student welfare organization Foundation for Student Life in Oslo, to subsidize kindergartens, health services, housing and cultural initiatives, the weekly newspaper *Universitas* and the radio station Radio Nova.

Jesuit: member of the Society of Jesus, the largest male Catholic religious order 耶稣会信徒

mural: wall painting

Imperial College of London: 帝国理工学院，伦敦大学(University of London)的独立学院

Royal institute of Technology: 皇家工学院，瑞典

Cornell University: 康奈尔大学，常春藤盟校中历史最短的一个

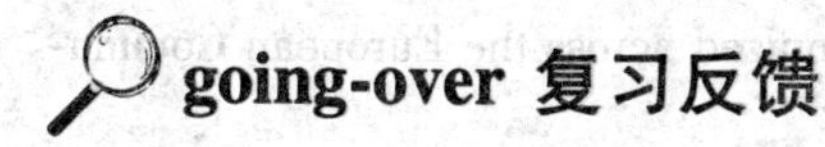

going-over 复习反馈

multiple-choice Q's

1. What institution of higher learning does not charge tuition fees?

A. The Eotvos Lorand University.

B. The National Autonomous University of Mexico.

C. The University of Oslo.

2. At what university was doctorate the only degree granted?

A. University of Zurich. B. University of Bologna.

C. University of Bergen.

3. Which university has the tallest educational building in the world?

A. Imperial College of London. B. Shanghai Jiao Tong University.

C. Lomonosov Moscow.

4. Whose main campus is a World Heritage site?

A. SJTU. B. UNAM. C. TTY.

5. ______ is university with Nobel Prize laureates among its alumni like Mario in Chemistry.

A. SJTU B. UNAM C. TTY

6. The seal of the University of ______ features Apollo with the Lyre.

A. Oslo B. Pennsylvania C. Madrid

7. Sometimes the local people refer to ______ by the name Poly.

A. UiO Blindern B. UC Berkeley C. ETH Zurich

8. The Faculty of Medicine is split between several university hospitals in the ______ area.

A. Oslo B. Pennsylvania C. Madrid

9. Which university is said to be founded as early as in 1088?

A. UNIBO B. ELTE C. TUT

essay Q's

10. How is higher education harmonized across the European Community?

11. Which universities do you think are ranked among the best in Europe?

12. Talk about the oldest and largest university in Hungary.

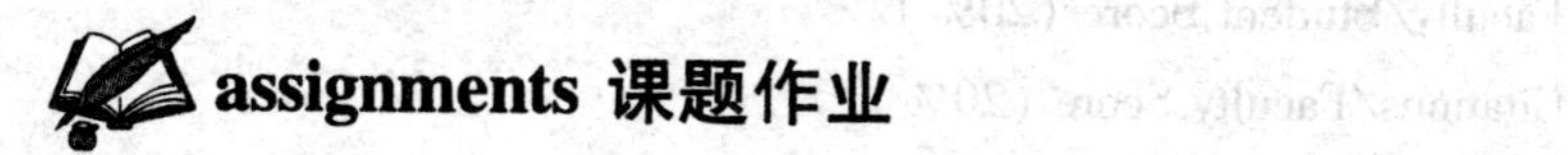

assignments 课题作业

Prepare a brief summary on Peiyang University (now Tianjin University). This assignment may be presented either as a written text or orally in class next time.

extensions 自主拓展

Learn after-class something about the university ranking system. This text is included mainly as entertainment. What's your comment on the issue, positive or critic?

Times Higher Education-QS World University Rankings was an annual publication that ranked the "Top 200 World Universities", and was published by Times Higher Education and Quacquarelli Symonds (QS) between 2004 and 2009. The full listings, which are broken down by subject and region, feature on the Times Higher Education website with the full 600 ranked universities, interactive rankings tables and detailed methodology published on the QS website. The best-known college and university rankings in the United States—compiled by US News & World Report—bases its "World's Best Universities" rankings on data from the Times Higher Education-QS World University Rankings.

The ranking weights are:

Peer Review Score (40%)

Recruiter Review (10%)

International Faculty Score (5%)

International Students Score (5%)

Faculty/Student Score (20%)

Citations/Faculty Score (20%).

After the 2009 rankings, Times Higher Education took the decision to end their relationship with QS and instead signed an agreement with Thomson Reuters to provide the data for its annual World University Rankings. Times Higher Education will develop a new rankings methodology in the coming months, in consultation with its readers, its editorial board and the firm. Thomson Reuters will collect and analyze the data used to produce the rankings on behalf of Times Higher Education. The results will be published annually from autumn 2010.

From November 2010, QS, who has bought the exclusive rights to the domain name of World University Rankings, will continue to produce them independently of Times Higher Education. These rankings will be produced using data collected and analyzed over the past six years by QS and Scopus by Elsevier.

Several universities in the UK and the Asia-Pacific region have commented on the rankings. Vice-Chancellor of Massey University, Professor Judith Kinnear says the Times Higher Education-QS ranking is a "wonderful external acknowledgement of several University attributes, including the quality of its research, research training, teaching and employability." She says the rankings are a true measure of a university's ability to fly high internationally: "The Times Higher Education ranking provides a rather more and more sophisticated, robust and well rounded measure of international and national ranking than either New Zealand's Performance Based Research Fund (PBRF) measure or the Shanghai rankings."

Ian Leslie, the pro-vice chancellor for research at Cambridge University said, "It is very reassuring that the collegiate systems of Cambridge and Oxford continue to be valued by and respected by peers, and that the excellence of teaching and of research at both institutions is reflected in these rankings."

The vice-chancellor of Oxford University, Dr. John Hood, said, "The exceptional talents of Oxford's students and staff are on display daily. This last year has seen many faculty members gaining national and international plaudits for their teaching, scholarship and research, and our motivated students continue to achieve in a number of fields, not just academically. Our place amongst the handful of truly world-class universities, despite the financial challenges we face, is testament to the quality and the drive of the members of this university's environment."

Vice-Chancellor of the University of Wollongong in Australia, Professor Gerard Sutton, said the ranking was a testament to a university's standing in the international community, identifying… "an elite group of world-class universities."

The rankings have been criticized for placing too much emphasis on peer review, which receives 40% of the overall score, and some have expressed concern about the manner in which the peer review has been carried out. It has also been criticized, by a member of the University of Auckland, New Zealand, for the volatility of its results, with results sometime "shifting markedly" year on year. Others have criticized the "opaque way it constructs its samples" for peer-review. Andrew Oswald has questioned the rankings on the basis that the respective league-table positions of the universities do not, at least in certain examples, correspond to the amount of Nobel Prizes they have recently won, arguing that "Stanford University in the United States, purportedly number 19 in the world, garnered three times as many Nobel Prizes over the past two decades as the universities of Oxford and Cambridge did combined."

However, several changes in methodology were introduced in 2007 which were aimed at addressing the above criticisms. But it has since been argued, in at least one paper, that the current method of peer-review is still insufficiently standardized, lacking "input data on any performance indicators".

Quacquarelli Symonds has been faulted for numerous data collection errors. For instance between 2006 and 2007 Washington University in St. Louis fell from 48th to 161st because QS mistakenly replaced Wash U with the University of Washington in Seattle. QS committed a similar error when collecting data for *Forbes Magazine* confusing the University of North Carolina's Kenan-Flagler business school with one from North Carolina Central University.

Some have argued that the Academic Ranking of World Universities by Shanghai Jiao Tong University may be more reliable, despite its perceived bias towards the natural sciences.

Commenting on Times Higher Education's decision to split from QS, editor Ann Mroz said, "universities deserve a rigorous, robust and transparent set of rankings—a serious tool for the sector, not just an annual curiosity." She went on to explain the reason behind the decision to continue to produce rankings without QS' involvement, saying that, "The responsibility weighs heavy on our shoulders... we feel we have a duty to improve how we compile them."

Quacquarelli Symonds: a company specializing in education and study abroad

be a testament to something: prove or show very clearly that something exists or is true

volatility: unpredictability

purportedly: supposedly

garner: take or collect

fault: criticize

参考答案
A's to Multiple-Choice Q's

Unit One

1. A 2. B 3. C 4. C 5. B
6. B 7. B 8. A 9. B

Unit Two

1. C 2. B 3. A 4. A 5. C
6. B 7. B 8. C 9. C

Unit Three

1. A 2. B 3. C 4. C 5. B
6. A 7. C 8. C 9. A

Unit Four

1. C 2. C 3. A 4. B 5. A
6. A 7. B 8. B 9. C

Unit Five

1. C 2. C 3. C 4. A 5. A
6. B 7. A 8. A 9. B

Unit Six

1. B 2. B 3. A 4. C 5. C
6. A 7. B 8. C 9. A

Unit Seven

1. B 2. B 3. A 4. C 5. A
6. C 7. A 8. B 9. C

Unit Eight

1. B 2. A 3. A 4. C 5. B
6. A 7. C 8. C 9. B

Unit Nine

1. B 2. B 3. B 4. C 5. A
6. A 7. C 8. A 9. C

Unit Ten

1. C 2. B 3. C 4. B 5. B
6. A 7. C 8. A 9. A